EMBRACING IRINA

LOVE WARS PREQUEL * ROSH HASHANAH HOLIDAY * NOVELLA

MICHELLE MARS

This book is dedicated to my Savta Leah who will never, ever, EVER read this book. My lineage, from her side of the family, hails from Azerbaijan and I drew some of Irina's strength of character, familial ties, and her if-you-come-for-me-I'm-taking-you-down attitude from my grandma. She is one tough cookie who loves fiercely and totally lets her grandchildren get away with things her children never could.
I love you, Savta Leah.

[1]

THE RECIPE

Irina's Bear-y Good Jewish Recipes Cookbook

Entry Four: Apples and Honey Tartlet with a Twist
Ingredients:

- 1 sheet puff pastry. Look at pg. 8 for recipe to make this. For those of you buying frozen…you monsters. Have you no pride? That's what I thought. Now go to pg. 8.
- 2 Golden Delicious apples prepped by peeling, coring, halving, and slicing thin. If you can see through it, too thin. If it breaks instead of bends, too thick.
- Honey. Can you ever have too much? (Hint: the answer is no, always no)
- 3-4 Tbs butter. Mmm. Mmm. Butter. Melted. (Do not use fake butter. Fake butter is crap. Are we making crap tartlets? I think not.)
- Cinnamon to taste
- 1 lemon, zested

Directions:

1. Line two baking sheets with parchment paper. Do not use foil. You know who you are. Now, roll out your prepared pastry sheet on a lightly floured surface. Make sure you get it nice and thin. It should end up being about a 16x12-inch rectangle.
2. Using a 6x6-inch square plate or cookie cutter, cut out four squares. Transfer two to each of the sheets. This would be a good time to send love to your pastry sheet, hoping you followed instructions correctly when making it. Cover and refrigerate for at least an hour. Ideally, a few hours, and for those that plan ahead, up to a day.
3. Put one rack near the top and one near the bottom of your oven so they have space to breathe and then preheat to 400°F.
4. This is the fun part. Get your apple slices into a bowl with the melted butter, a bunch of honey, and the cinnamon. Toss to coat them well. Try not to eat them along the way. Consider it a challenge.
5. Next, take your prepared slices and overlap them, evenly distributing them among all four squares, leaving about a 1/4-inch border. Drizzle your excess butter and honey mixture over the apples.
6. Once your oven is ready, and not before, place them in. Bake until your pastry is golden and your apples are nice and tender, about 22-28 minutes.
7. While your puffy goodness is baking, take more honey and stir it in a bowl with your lemon zest. Leave it to sit and infuse. This stuff is so good on anything, feel free to make extra and place it in the refrigerator for later.
8. After you pull your sheets out of the oven, take your lemon honey and drizzle it over all four squares. Okay, fine… You can drizzle some on your tongue too, but only once the squares are properly covered in decorative lines.

9. Finally, transfer your tartlets to cooling racks and let cool for about 5-7 minutes. You won't make it beyond that before you feel the need to eat them.
10. Pro tip: Serve warm with a scoop of vanilla ice cream drizzled with your lemon honey and a glass of medovukha. This honey-based alcohol is always a good idea, but especially for Rosh Hashanah and while eating these tartlets.

Always serve with love,
Irina

CHAPTER 1

Redwood City, CA
September 2025

Irina Rivkin put the final touches to her newest menu item, her Apples and Honey Tartlet. It was the embodiment of two things she adored, the fall and Rosh Hashanah. This year, above all previous years, her family was going into the holiday with extra determination to make it memorable. After all, this might well be the last time they were able to celebrate on Earth.

Ever since the aliens, known as the Staraban, had arrived spreading pamphlets and agreeing to press interviews, things had been a bit strained. They claimed that the Earth was dying and that they came to relocate humans to a New Earth and, frankly, not everyone believed them. First contact hadn't been as bad as the movies always predicted, but...relocating all of humanity away from Earth? It hadn't gone too well either.

Like many around the planet, the Rivkin family was pretty much glued to the news. It was important to stay informed when you could find yourself on a one-way ticket off the planet. Of course, her family had already experienced relocation, ages before, when they fled from what was once the Russian Empire due to religious persecutions also known as pogroms. For Irina, until it was their time to relocate, she was going to continue to run her little bakery in the heart of Redwood City, California. It gave her too much pleasure to do anything else. And for those worried about the move, nothing can calm a body like baked goods. Her business had been doing just fine despite the disruption expected.

For this high-holiday season, her whole family was still on Earth and having to face the question, "What if this is the last Rosh Hashanah they celebrated on this planet?" That could potentially mean no more apples and honey, for instance, which were a big part of the celebration. Who knew what kinds of plants and critters they would find on New Earth? Even if they brought seedlings and bees and all the rest, Noah's ark style, who knew if they would take to this new planet and how long it might be before they saw the fruits of said labor? So, this year, they were going all out.

To that end, Irina added the new tartlet item to her bakery shop and her cookbook. She adored baking, being her own boss, and filling her customers' bellies with tasty treats that brought a smile to their faces. She only hoped that after an adjustment period and learning curve, she would be able to do so on New Earth. She was considering whether she should keep the same name and mascot, "Bear-y Good Bakery" with the cutest brown bear in an apron—adorable, if she did say so herself, and also a bit of an inside joke—or come up with something new.

Focusing back on what she was doing, she finished sprinkling the tarts with a touch of powdered sugar. With the Jewish New Year looming only a couple of weeks away, she was excited to see how her customers reacted to it. She had used the customary honey, for a sweet year ahead, and apples, for a bountiful one too, and threw in some twists to make her own taste-bud-entrancing, baked yumminess. They could all use those blessings to face the new adventure ahead.

As she brought out the new confection, the bell over her front door chimed. Her mouth, watering from the smells coming out of her kitchen only a moment before, suddenly went very dry. Her smile grew—probably ridiculously—wider and her pulse raced. In the doorway stood one of her favorite customers. Of course, she'd never told Kesh how she felt, but over the course of the last three months, the Staraban warrior had been coming in every few days, which thrilled Irina to no end.

Every time Irina saw her, she couldn't help but absorb every detail about the lovely alien. Kesh was tall, as were all the Staraban, and had a sleek, muscular physique. Her golden, almost yellow-ish skin was lovely to behold, and her lavender-hued eyes were often crinkled with humor. She had delicate features marred—or enhanced, depending on your perspective—by a scar along her cheek and across her mouth.

Irina'd had some very titillating dreams about that mouth.

Irina's hand shook. The impact of Kesh on her senses was an impressive thing that she had never dealt with from anyone else. Mentally and physically, there was no denying her instant awareness of Kesh the moment she walked into a room. To cover it up, she kneeled down to place the tray of tarts into her display, breaking contact before she made a fool of herself. She looked up and found Kesh standing just on the other side of the counter.

Was she staring at Irina's ass? Heat climbed up her neck and, with her fair complexion, it would be evident to anyone glancing in that general direction. Whether from embarrassment or desire, unknown, but she could give her warming oven a run for its money. But this was no way to greet a customer. *Get it together, Irina!* Maybe she could stick her head into the cooler instead of the tarts?

That was not to be, though, as Kesh began talking, and it would be rude to stay down below, right?

"How are you doing today, Irina? Whatever you just brought out smells delicious."

She stood and met Kesh's eyes as she replied noting the warmth there. *Warmth?* It distracted her enough that her words tumbled out one on top of the other like playful bear cubs. "Good morning,

Kesh. I'm great. And, yes, it is delicious. Would you like one? How are you?"

The alien appeared to lean forward a fraction more—or was that in Irina's imagination?—and directed a sexy smirk her way. The twist to Kesh's mouth, with her scar, made her look like a dangerous, golden, pirate. And Irina was so very here for it. Or, she would be, if this wasn't her customer, and an alien, and someone unlikely to want to have anything to do with humans. "I am well. Things are now moving relatively smoothly with relocation. Less fighting makes relocation so much easier. Only a few resistance groups left that we are trying to negotiate or subdue. The biggest is HARM, and they are mostly non-violent as far as we can tell."

"The Humans Against Relocation Movement?"

"Yes. That one."

"I hope you can come to a resolution soon."

"Me too. We are not usually met with resistance when we offer our assistance. Of course, this has been handled a bit—" Kesh hesitated, which wasn't like the warrior, and gave Irina the impression she might not continue or perhaps said too much, but then the warrior began talking again, "—differently than most of our commissions so I suppose some resistance might have been anticipated."

"How do you usually handle these things?"

"We would wait for a species to approach us themselves. Strangely, humans have chosen not to focus much of their energy and technology toward space travel. We were concerned, based on the scientific findings we had about Earth, that humans would not achieve it in time to have us save them. So we came despite traditional commission procedures. We just want to help."

"I admit that my family considered joining the resistance, but then I met you, and I have a good sense about people, er, individuals. You convinced me you weren't here to harm us." Was that more warmth she saw coming from Kesh? A girl can dream and a bear could smell and what she was smelling coming from Kesh was—

"And, I would love one."

"One what?" Irina just blinked. *One what?*

Kesh gave her pirate smirk again and said, "One of the things you just brought from your kitchen."

"Oh. Right. Of course." *You are a baker. She is your customer. You serve customers baked goods. Now get it together.*

"I would also like your tea."

"My special blend?"

"Yes."

"Okay." Irina placed one of the tartlets on a plate, placed it in front of Kesh with a napkin, and assembled the herbs she liked to blend for her "Bear-y Good Morning" tea. It made for nearly as good a kick in the pants as coffee, but actually lasted longer. From behind her, Kesh kept talking, though it sounded like she had her mouth full.

"This is—mmm—so crunchy—mmm—and sweet and tart—mmm—and so good. I could eat your baking all day. This reminds me that I have been meaning to ask you something."

"Okay." Irina turned and placed the tea in front of Kesh. "That will be $8.50."

Kesh handed her a ten-dollar bill, and with a non-piratic-yet-still-toe-curling smile, said in a husky voice, "No change."

Irina's heart flipped. Not because of the tip, though that was nice, but that huskiness undid Irina. Her top teeth dug into her bottom lip as she sealed her mouth. There was no way she was going to allow herself another explosion of word vomit. Instead, she swallowed down words like alphabet soup and tilted her head slightly in gratitude. One point for the self-control column. Near thing since she could have sworn Kesh's eyes had stared hungrily at her lips for the briefest moment when her teeth had made an appearance. She was probably just reading what she wanted into the situation.

Kesh continued speaking breaking into Irina's musings, "Would you be willing to have your recipes put into our Food Delivery Assistant?"

"Your what?"

"Our food replicators? The FDAs? Have you not seen any yet?

No." Kesh answered herself. "You have not. You have not been on our base nor in our ships. My mista—"

"Let me stop you there. I think I get the idea, and the answer is absolutely not." Irina tried to think of it from the alien's point of view, but really, she couldn't. No one was going to take her recipes. Not without buying her goddamn cookbook. And even then, to think that her recipes could be made by some machine that "replicated" food. Hell. No. Still, she cared about Kesh, so she did temper her response, a tiny itsy bitsy bit. Instead of saying, "You can take that idea and shove it up your asshole," she said, "My recipes are not for replicating," and tried not to sound quite as offended as she felt. She must have failed, based on Kesh's response.

"I am very sorry if I have offended you."

She totally had.

"I did not mean to."

Irina knew that.

"Please forgive me."

Anything. Irina would forgive her anything. That was when Irina took note of the fact that with each stammered phrase, she and Kesh had both leaned closer together over the counter. She was now staring directly up into the stunning warrior's eyes from only inches away.

She meant to say "Okay," but nothing came out. Her mouth moved, but words failed her. Irina could feel Kesh's breath along her own lips, and it sent tingles down her spine. It would only take lifting up on her toes and she would be able to lean in those last couple of inches and finally feel the press of those lips she'd been desiring for so long. Kesh's nose flared a little and she looked down. Was she thinking about Irina's lips too? It seemed like she might be.

Without thinking it through, Irina licked her lips, moistening them, and heard Kesh's swift inhale of breath. Her following exhale cooled the dampness still clinging there. And against her heated skin, it was divine. Like a caress. When Kesh mimicked Irina's lip licking, Irina wanted to follow the same path with her own tongue.

She imagined dripping honey onto those lips and using just her mouth to clean them up. How decadent would it feel? Her mind conjured up all sorts of great places she wanted to cover in honey and lick on Kesh. In fact, hadn't Kesh just been eating her tartlet? She would taste like honey right now. Irina growled low in her throat. Well, shit. Growling at the customers was definitely not in the customer service manual. She should withdraw. Walk backward. At the very least, lean backward. She really, really should.

[2]

HAPPY

Irina's Bear-y Good Jewish Recipes Cookbook

Notes for Rosh Hashanah
Recipes I need to include:

Round challah with dead grapes and without. Explain the many
reasons behind the roundness of it. Godly crown. Yearly cycle. That
repentance is always available year-round. Wouldn't it be nice if the
rabbis could just choose one interpretation? They're all good
though, so… include them all.
Pomegranate-mandarin orange parfait. Mention the seeds being the
good deeds for the coming year, but also that it's a kickass recipe full
of antioxidants and vitamin C for the health nuts.

Maybe develop a few more recipes with the apples and honey. Can't
have enough honey.

Make sure to sign off with
Always serve with love,
Irina

CHAPTER 2

Redwood City, CA
June 2025

Three months earlier…

Kesh had not known what to expect when ARC, the Alien Relocation Cooperative, chose to relocate the humans off of Earth. She was a communications specialist and had studied every alien species that was a part of the All Alien Alliance. Unfortunately, the humans were not a part of AAA so she had spent the time between taking the commission and implementing it, studying every piece of information she was able to get her hands on. She had added all of the Earth languages to their translator implants. Learned about the various cultures and what might appeal to humans as a form of contact. In fact, she had helped to come up with the pamphlet idea in the first place.

Despite all of this, the humans rebelled. Not all of the humans, but various groups formed. The violent ones needed to be subdued for the safety of everyone and they attempted to use as little force as possible to do it. The more difficult were those that hid and were trying to bring down the aliens' attempts at peaceful relocation from hidden means like **HARM**.

Her job was to monitor every piece of intelligence that came in to help figure out what their agenda was and where they were located. It was clear that, just as ARC had chosen to put their main base near the area called Silicon Valley because some of the biggest, richest, and most socially influential companies on Earth were located there, so too was **HARM** in the vicinity.

When she was not working though, Kesh loved going out into the human cities, especially the most peaceful areas, and learning more about the culture in a personal experience capacity. She had no idea at the time that her walk through the shops of Redwood City would impact her life so completely. She spotted a bakery with a human animal called a bear in the window and since she was hungry for a small meal, approached it.

Right away, before even entering the facility, her mouth began to water. The smell of baked goods surrounded her as she stood in front of the door. She looked in the window and her mouth began to water for a whole different reason. Moving around inside was the most beautiful female Kesh had ever seen. The human was big with enchanting curves that made Kesh's hands flex to touch. She could make out short-cropped hair of a light shade and stern features.

There was no question that she would be going in now. When she opened the door, the bell that rang startled her briefly and when she turned back toward the female, her dual hearts skipped beats. With no glass separating them, she could now tell that the female's hair was darker at the scalp and with honey-blond highlights throughout. It was a little longer near the front as it swooped over her dark brows.

Her stern features softened as she smiled, welcoming Kesh in. The Staraban would bet that her smiles, besides for her customers, would come sparingly, which is exactly the kind of thing to draw Kesh in. She would take hard-won smiles, any day over those given out like rain drops. Those smiles are always more beautiful to her for their rareness. And then, Kesh met the female's eyes and was completely dazzled by the green. By their direct, honest, and assessing gaze. It would appear she might not be the only one cataloguing features. Did that mean this human would be interested in her? It was hard to fathom with how the humans had reacted, as a whole, to the Staraban.

But… If she was interested, something inside Kesh told her this was someone a warrior could rely on.

September 2025

Present day…

When she first walked into the bakery, she had not realized that today would be the day that something would change between them. She had been waiting for a moment like this to present itself for three months. Way too long. Then Irina had bent over, giving Kesh the most beautiful view of her gorgeous round ass, and waiting any longer seemed an impossibility.

She probably should have felt guilty having been caught staring at Irina's butt. She should have, but mostly she had felt lust as she imagined, not for the first time, how Irina's ass would feel in her hands. Of course all guilt became irrelevant now that they were standing in such proximity that they were breathing each other's air.

So close. So deliciously close. Almost as close as she had always dreamed of them being.

She took a deep breath, letting Irina's scent infuse her system. Yes. She wanted this baker more than she had wanted anyone before. No one's scent had ever smelled so right; like a walk in the woods tinged with sweetness and something wild. Then, Irina licked her lips, and Kesh felt lost to her basest predatory instincts.

Her inhale was completely involuntary, as was complying with the need to lick her own lips in response. When Irina growled at her, it was the sexiest thing Kesh had ever heard. All thoughts of where they were, what they had been talking about, and proper behavior for a Staraban representative vanished. She took note the moment Irina's body language changed, and she could tell the baker was about to pull back.

She did not want that. Not now that they were finally here. Three months she had visited and longed to touch this female and she was not about to wait another minute. Someone had to make the first move and Kesh was just the alien to do it. Taking charge was something she was quite comfortable doing.

"Kiss me, Irina."

Irina stilled at her command. That was a good sign. The look of surprise tinged in hope was also a good sign.

Irina's voice, usually so sure, came out a whisper. "Are…are you sure? Do you want this too?"

"Do not make me tell you again. If you want me, then kiss me."

Kesh was a rather laid back, easy-going warrior, but in bed she owned the room, her partner, and both their pleasure. She found it best to start as she planned to continue. With Irina being such a strong-willed human whose personality filled a room, Kesh had always worried that they would not be compatible in this way. But Irina's eyes dilated at her command, and she leaned up, pressing her lips to Kesh's mouth.

It was a sweet, tentative tasting. Their lips holding their own conversation.

I have wanted you for so long.
Is this happening?
You feel so soft.
Where is this going?
You taste so good.

Kesh wanted more. She brought her hand up and around Irina's neck, gripping her firmly, drawing her slowly in, but giving her a chance to put a stop to things if she wished. Irina did not pull away. Set free to move forward, Kesh brought her other hand around the other side of Irina's neck and used her thumb to tilt her head up and slightly to the side. Then, using the same thumb, she applied a gentle pressure on her chin, and satisfaction hit her as Irina understood and complied by opening her mouth.

Gentle was not her style, so Kesh thrust her tongue between Irina's open lips, tasting her deeply. She poured three months of desire and longing into the kiss so there would be no doubt in Irina's mind what Kesh wanted. Irina stiffened momentarily, probably surprised at the ferocity of her claiming, but the baker rallied quickly, and her whole being seemed to soften in Kesh's hands. Her lips went pliant yet hungry and the weight of her head pillowed in Kesh's palms. It was everything.

A noise from outside the shop reminded Kesh that this was not the time or place for anything more, so she slowly eased back, placing a chaste kiss on the corner of Irina's mouth and running her cheek along Irina's cheek feeling the softness of her skin. She whispered in Irina's ear, "I want to see you later."

Irina answered her breathlessly, huskily, "Yes. I close at five thirty this evening. Can you come here then?"

"Yes. And, again, I regret asking about the replicator."

"Perhaps tonight, you will let me teach you how to bake something and you will see why it cannot be replicated."

"I would enjoy that."

Kesh trailed her lips along Irina's jawline and enjoyed how her responsive human's pulse began to race instantly. The gasp that came from her lips was an added gift. Kesh gave her one more brief, demanding kiss and then pulled away. She slowly eased her hands from around Irina's throat and came back up to her full height. She could not help the gratified smirk as she watched Irina blink herself back into her body. She planned to make her even more senseless that evening. Irina would be a puddle of pleasure if Kesh had her way.

She patiently waited but was surprised when Irina finally collected herself and said, "Everything is on the house."

"What? What does that mean?"

Irina cleared her throat and when she spoke again, her voice was back to her direct tone. "It means that your coffee and pastry will cost you nothing. Take whatever you wish."

"But I already paid."

"Oh. Right." Clearly flustered, Irina opened the register and placed the same ten-dollar bill back on the counter near Kesh's plate.

Kesh planned to take a lot, but not from the café. Her voice sounded rough even to her own ears as she simply said, "Thank you."

"You're welcome. Do you need to run, or will you be staying here to eat?"

Kesh had planned to sit in the café, but that was before that kiss. She figured it would be better and safer to leave until later tonight. "I need to get back to the base. I will see you later."

Irina gave her a smile, and Kesh's day warmed in verifiable degrees. "Until later, then."

With that, Kesh took the last bite of her pastry in one hand, her tea in the other, and left, leaving the money behind. She had some work to complete so she could come back on time that evening. And when she came back, Irina might be teaching her to bake, but Kesh was going to be the one teaching a lesson about heat. No doubt Irina had experience, but alongside all the alien cultural traditions she had studied, she had also made a personal study of various sexual practices. Sex was just another language after all.

[3]

SWEET

Irina's Bear-y Good Jewish Recipes Cookbook

Notes for Rosh Hashanah

Recipes I need to include – of the non-traditional variety:

Sweet potato fries and maple pashteedah. Double-check the egg and
cheese ratio. Telling them, "Until it's the right consistency," won't
work. Also double-check on the cooking time. People who read
recipe books need such ridiculous details. "Cook until it's done you
bastards," doesn't sell well.

Pomegranate-pinkened bagels with a honey-walnut cream cheese.
This falls under the Yom Kippur breaking of the fast section. Don't
forget to move it there when you start working on it because you
know you will.

Whipped honey cream-cheese filled kreplach in an apple, banana,
and chia seed smoothie "soup." People are going to think you've hit

your head with this recipe but just wait until they see the Passover
section.

These notes are leaving me hungry all the time. Do I really want to
write this cookbook?

Always serve with love,
Irina

CHAPTER 3

Redwood City, CA
September 2025

Irina hadn't been this nervous or excited since she went through her first bear shift when she was still a cub. The anticipation and longing blended into a cocktail inside her body much like the herbs in her morning tea. She felt so fucking alive. Something about Kesh told her that Irina was never going to be the same after tonight. Just like after that first shift.

She lumbered with extra verve around her kitchen, tidying up and preparing all of the ingredients they would need. She had spent much of the day angsting over which treat to make. It was definitely a hard call. It needed to be something not too sweet, but not too savory. Something just right. When she realized she sounded like fucking Goldilocks, she quickly made up her mind and moved on to prep. She couldn't help reliving their earlier kiss though. Kesh had tasted of honey, and that already would have been so delicious, but she also tasted of strength, passion, and a unique flavor all her own.

Irina was in deep.

Who was she kidding? She had been in deep since first sight and smell.

June 2025

Three months earlier…

Irina had just put some of her most desirable summer cookies, the piña colada cookie crumble, in her display case when the bell rang over her door. She stood rooted to the ground like an ancient sequoia. Luckily, there was a brief moment, as the alien was startled and looked up at the bell, for Irina to pull herself together. She couldn't decide what was most concerning. The fact that one of the aliens just stepped into her bakery, or the fact that the instant the alien walked in, Irina wanted to jump over her counter to smell her up close and personal. She smelled divine.

Instead of revealing her bear skills to accomplish jumping over her counter, she smiled and welcomed her in. From there, despite what her body kept urging her to do, Irina served the alien some tea and a few different baked items. If it nearly hurt not to reach out and touch her, well, that was for Irina to know and battle.

She dreamed of golden skin, lavender eyes, and scarred lips wrapping themselves around her…cookies that night. When she woke up the next morning, it had been necessary to make the time for some self-love before she showered and headed in to start baking before the café opened.

It seemed like such a good idea too until, unexpectedly, the same alien walked in a few short hours later and Irina couldn't help the blush she was sure stained her cheeks. *Fuck! Relax. Relax. It's not like the aliens are mind readers. She doesn't know what you did and who you thought about this morning!* She was giving herself good advice, but it didn't help her one bit. She kept her eyes downcast and her body busy the whole time the alien had been there.

The next day, her morning started in much the same way. The likelihood the gorgeous alien would come back, yet again, a third day in a row was super slim. Especially true after Irina's standoffish behavior.

When the morning came and went with no sign of the Staraban, her stomach clenched in regret. What would she do if she never saw her again? *Go on with your life, of course. As though an alien had any use for a human.*

It had been a particularly busy day, but there was a lull in customers, so Irina went in the back to get some of the tea blends to refill the dwindling ones up front when she heard her bell. She rushed out carrying the ones she'd already gathered and came face-to-face with her alien. Technically not hers, but it was hard to remember that when her body practically vibrated with need. She stammered out her greeting and turned to deposit all of her tea on the counter.

Tingles ran down her spine as the alien's rich voice replied. "Hello."

The word was like a caress along her nerves. She spun back, "What can I get for you today?"

"I will take one of your muffins and the breakfast blend."

"Which muffin are you in the mood for?" At least her voice sounded steady and she wasn't rambling.

"Surprise me."

Had that sounded a bit like a command? She thought so and certain parts of her grew damp almost immediately.

"I would also like a breakfast tea."

"Sure thing."

That was about the extent of their conversations for the last couple of days. She expected that would stay true then as well. True until the Staraban kept talking. "Are you the owner of this bakery?"

"Yes."

"May I have your name?"

"Yes. Of course. I'm Irina and you?"

"Kesh."

Kesh. Sigh. Her dreams now had a name for her to yell out. This wasn't good. Obsession-ville, ticket for one please.

And so it went over the next weeks and months. With every interaction and every conversation causing Irina to have more elaborate fantasies about one certain alien. After Kesh described her position in ARC, Irina pictured her speaking filthy things in a multitude of gibberish-to-Irina languages. When Kesh mentioned an alien culture that had a ritualistic body paint celebration, Irina pictured painting the warrior in chocolate blended with honeycomb bits and edible gold leaf. One day Kesh arrived at the same time that the bakery received its supply shipments and proved just how strong she was by lifting some of the heavier boxes by herself in an effort to help out. Irina spent that night picturing herself being lifted up against a wall.

Outwardly, Irina stayed friendly and unphased. Inwardly, she was drowning in desire. She took to wearing two underwear on some days to deal with how wet Kesh made her.

On top of her longing there was also anxiety, which made each interaction precious. What if she was relocated and never saw her warrior again?

September 2025

Present day…

A knock came from the front door, which roused Irina out of her reverie. She rushed out of the kitchen, and sure enough, there was Kesh behind the locked door. She might be closed for business, but they had anything but business planned for the night.

She made her way to the door, her eyes never wavering from Kesh's intense gaze. Like the rays of the sun, it heated her skin clear through the glass. In fact, it wouldn't have surprised her to see the glass melting from such a look. Why hadn't she turned up the air conditioning? Oh, yeah. She already kept it quite cool in the bakery. *You don't need AC, you need an ice bath.*

She stepped back as she opened the door, allowing Kesh to walk in, and then pushed it closed. As she went to lock it again, multiple things happened all at once. Kesh had the door locked and spun Irina around, while also pressing her firmly against it. How many hands does this alien have? She could have sworn there were only two, but boy was she efficient and fast with them.

Some indignant part of Irina wanted to protest the rough handling, but who was she kidding? She loved it. Her sputtering thoughts and her wet pussy were proof enough of the effect Kesh had on her. She opened her mouth to say…well, something, but Kesh bent down before any consonant or vowel could escape and licked at Irina's lower lip. Words. Who needed them? What were words anyway when you had lip licking to succumb to?

Kesh murmured between licks, "I have missed these lips all day. Tell me I can have them now. Do not make me wait any longer."

"Yes."

Well, at least she found one word. The only word she needed right then.

Kesh didn't miss even a moment. The "s" in her "yes" was hissed directly into Kesh's mouth as the alien laid claim to Irina. At least, that was how it felt. She felt conquered. Her knees even went weak. What self-respecting bear had weak knees? Who could blame her though? The alien didn't taste of honey now. She tasted like raw power and sensuality.

As intense as it was, and as fast as it came about, the kiss was over in an instant. Kesh, breathing heavy, voice deeper than usual, said, "Thank you. I needed that. Now, I am ready to be your kitchen student," with a surprisingly bashful smile on her kiss-plump and wet lips.

Irina had only one response to that once she caught her breath. "Oy. That was quite a greeting. I…uh…think I need an iced tea. No. I know I do. You?"

"I will have what you are having. I do not think I have tried your iced tea. I am sure I will like it."

They silently drank as their eyes promised hot, naughty things. When they finished drinking, Irina headed toward the door separating the kitchen from the front. "Shall we?"

"Yes."

Kesh had said that yes in such a sexy purr, Irina almost dropped her glass. She was suddenly exceedingly relieved she had chosen a relatively easy recipe to make. They might actually succeed in making something by the time they finished using all of the ingredients she so wisely already had measured and laid out. *Thank you, past Irina!*

"What are we making? Your apple and honey pastry from earlier?"

"No, but we are sticking with the theme, because Rosh Hashanah is around the corner."

"And what is Rosh Hashanah?"

"Hmm. I'm not sure how much studying you have done on our religions and cultures, but I am Jewish, and Rosh Hashanah is the Jewish New Year. The beginning of the next year in the Jewish calendar. It also begins an important set of holidays we call the High Holidays." Irina watched as Kesh's focus wavered. That was enough info dump. "I'll get you a book about it if you want."

"I would enjoy that, it sounds familiar, but your planet has many cultures with many traditions to study. I have not learned much about this tradition."

"Understandable. Anyway, to make a long story short, to celebrate the New Year we use a lot of apples and honey in our foods. The apples represent a wish for a fruitful next year and the honey a wish for a sweet year."

"What a beautiful and delicious tradition. I enjoyed those flavors immensely earlier. What are we doing with them now?"

"I prepped some of the longer, harder steps or we might be here working for hours, but we will be making apple cinnamon rolled cookies with a crushed honeycomb vanilla ice cream on top. The ice cream, I already made and froze. I also prepared the roll. What we are going to need to do is cut the roll, bake it, sprinkle it, and top it." Kesh's eyes did that thing where she lost focus again, so Irina wrapped it up. "We'll take it step by step."

"That is a good idea. I have not had a reason to try to bake before. We have our FDAs. The Staraban probably cooked once upon a time, but it is not something we do much anymore." Kesh smiled sheepishly and Irina wanted to snuggle into her. As high as the heat between them blazed, sometimes all a person wanted was some comfort. She wanted to assure her alien that it would be okay because she got the impression that Kesh rarely found herself out of her depth. And so she did exactly that.

She walked over and wrapped Kesh in her bear hug, and as Kesh's arms came around Irina's shoulders, she felt the tension flow right out of her alien as her muscles relaxed. Actually, out of them both. Between Kesh and her kitchen, Irina was home. How odd since this wouldn't be her home for much longer if Kesh's alien company had its way and she was relocated. Irina had to consider that perhaps it wasn't a geographic location that was giving her that feeling.

She could have stayed in Kesh's arms forever, but she was also excited to share her passion for food with someone that mattered to her. After months of getting to know Kesh and admiring her, Kesh mattered.

Once again, Irina had the feeling that after tonight she wouldn't be the same. As if Kesh's very presence had begun, over the months of their acquaintance, to terraform Irina to nurture a new way of life. A life that would hopefully sustain a relationship with her beloved alien. She was ready for it. This bear ran away from nothing.

[4]

NEW

Irina's Bear-y Good Jewish Recipes Cookbook

Notes on my intro:
Talk about what growing up Jewish meant to you.

Discuss the intrinsic role that food plays in Jewish celebrations.

Somehow avoid talking about being a shifter while also highlighting
the importance of honey in all things, because honey.

Alcohol. Enough said.
Weave in a joke or two. Yeah. Be funny. You can do it.

Highlight the importance of making things from scratch. These
bakers today are always taking shortcuts. Make them see the light of
day, ~~but don't belittle them too much~~. Do your best.

Try to be brief. Less is more and all that.
Always serve with love,
Irina

CHAPTER 4

Redwood City, CA
September 2025

Kesh had it bad. At least, that was the Earth phrase that came to mind. She found herself smooshed between the hardness of the counter and the softness of Irina's body as her distraction did her best to teach Kesh how big to slice each cookie off the roll so they would cook evenly. It was not just the feel of her that was the problem. The scent of sweet apples and cinnamon coming off of the dough in front of her mixed with Irina's scent behind her, and all of that overlaid by the scent of their mutual arousal was nearly too much. How was she expected to concentrate on cutting something when all she wanted to do was grab that tantalizing morsel, throw her to the ground, and bury her face in her abundant breasts? Goddess help her persevere.

"You've got it."

Irina's words praised her, but she felt punished as the baker moved away.

"I'll just grab us the cookie sheet so we can place them."

Kesh would like to place her somewhere and make sure she

would not be able to move away.

"Here it is. You can see I lined it with parchment paper, which will help us to remove them after they bake."

She would remove the apron first and then lift up her dress and remove her underwear.

"I can't wait for you to taste these. I added a little wine to the apple mixture as it cooked, giving it sweetness, but also an earthy flavor."

She wanted to taste something, but it was Irina's pussy her mouth watered for at the moment.

"And once we put the honey ice cream on top, it will be like an explosion of taste in your mouth."

She wanted to taste the explosion of Irina's orgasm.

"Are you still paying attention? You're staring at me and haven't moved to put the cookies on the sheet. Is this boring you?" Kesh refocused because Irina's voice sounded irritated and stern. Clearly, she needed to get her libido back under control. Irina was sharing something that was important to her with Kesh, and the baker had every right to be angry at her inattention.

"I am sorry. I will do a better job ignoring my desire for you and pay attention to what you are showing me."

The most lovely shade of pink crawled up Irina's neck and cheeks. She stopped herself from noticing for too long or she would find herself distracted again. Instead, she began placing the rounds she had cut on the baking sheet. "Like this?"

"Yes. Exactly." Irina's voice was back to sounding warm and inviting. Good.

She finished, and Irina showed her how the oven worked and said they would need to wait fifteen minutes for the cookies to bake. When she turned back to her, Kesh was back to wanting to grab her, but she did not want to make the same mistake as before so instead she said, "What do you want me to do next?"

Irina took her hand and walked her over to a counter near the back corner. She then jumped up onto it, pulling Kesh close between her legs. "I want to mess around while we wait. Does that work for you?"

Kesh did not feel the need to answer with words. She maneuvered their joined hands behind Irina's back, forcing her to sit tall and bringing her up against Kesh's chest. With her other hand, she cradled the back of Irina's head, holding her in place. Her earlier thoughts had her moving quick, but now that she was here, Kesh chose to move slow.

She brought her lips to Irina's ear, feeling the soft skin of her cheek as it heated against her own. She licked the outer curve and then bit on her lobe. She proceeded to trail a row of kisses down Irina's neck. The baker's heavy breathing, interrupted by quick inhales of breath and then followed by nearly silent rumblings she felt against her lips, told Kesh how much this affected her adored. When she reached the juncture of her neck and shoulder, she bit. Irina's pulse stuttered and then raced.

"I want to mark you here. May I mark you?"

Irina sounded a bit concerned when she answered. "Do you mean like a hickey? There isn't some alien marking thing I should know about that never goes away and lets you drag me back with you or something?"

Kesh could not help laughing. She released Irina and placed both her palms flat on the counter on either side of the female's hips. "No." She laughed some more, her forehead landing on the baker's shoulder. "No, sweet Irina. We do not permanently mark our lovers and take them home as some form of property. I meant I wanted to suck on your skin and bite you until there would be a rush of blood there that would leave a mark. Is that a—what did you call it?" She lifted her head to look into Irina's eyes.

"Hickey."

"Yes. That. May I hickey you?"

Irina giggled. Her sweet but stern human actually giggled. "Yes. You may hickey me as much as you want as long as I can wear clothing over them. I can't have my customers and family see me covered in them all up and down my neck. But…" Irina's voice grew huskier, no giggling in sight as she continued, "anywhere else is acceptable."

Her insides were all twisted up in desire at that tone. "Understood, lovely. I look forward to finding all those places I can mark you."

"Good, then, um…would you please continue what you were doing?"

"Since you are asking so nicely, how can I resist?" She used one hand to pull Irina's top to the side and the other to cradle the back of her neck. She ran her nose along the side of her neck, following the path she had licked a few moments before. And just where she had stopped earlier, she began to lick and bite at Irina. "I believe this is the spot where I stopped. The spot I wanted to mark. It is a really nice spot, but as enticing as this spot is…" She licked a bit farther into the juncture to the area she had exposed when pulling the top over. "This spot right here…"

She bit and sucked hard at the soft skin between her lips. Heard Irina's indrawn breath as the baker's strong hands gripped Kesh's sides. Smelled her arousal coming from between her spread legs as it blended with her own around them. She lifted her lips far enough so she could see the evidence of her lust manifest, and it was beautiful. *This human is mine. She is mine, and I am hers.* Satisfaction lodged in Kesh's throat. She had never experienced anything like her feelings for Irina. Hoping that was true for the baker too, she looked into her eyes.

Heat, longing, and affection shone there. For her. "Sweet Irina. I have wanted to claim you as mine for months. May I keep touching you? I want to bring you as much pleasure and satisfaction as I feel just looking at my mark on you."

Irina gave one of her rare smiles, and Kesh wanted to fall to her knees from the impact. "I would like that very much, but—"

Kesh's hearts raced with concern over that "but." Irina did not want her to touch…But before her thought could run away with her, Irina continued. "The cookies will need to come out of the oven within the next minute. Later?"

Relief was a palatable taste in Kesh's mouth. The cookies. Of course. "Later. I plan to feast on more than cookies and ice cream."

[5]

YEAR

Irina's Bear-y Good Jewish Recipes Cookbook

Notes on savory baked goods for Rosh Hashanah:

Honey mustard, phyllo-wrapped salmon pockets. Figure out how to talk about fish heads as the "head" of the year and connection with "Rosh" meaning head without turning squeamish people's stomachs. Can't exactly tell them to turn into a bear and go to the nearest river and fish. Talk about how many now just make a fish dish to represent since heads are not a thing most people eat anymore, hence this recipe. You can't even write the notes on this one without it getting long. Good luck.

Brisket pot pie. Because brisket.

Sweet potato bourekas with a spicy honey dip. May need to go make these tasty pockets of goodness for dinner tonight.

Always serve with love,
Irina

CHAPTER 5

Redwood City, CA
September 2025

Irina passed the next few moments in a daze. Apparently, at some point, she had removed the cookies from the oven, set them to cool slightly, showed Kesh the honeycomb vanilla ice cream and how to scoop it, arranged a couple of plates for them, plated the cookies, watched as Kesh scooped a mound of one on the other, and for the final touch, drizzled some honey over it all. Her mouth was watering, but as delicious as her new dish looked, she didn't think that it was the reason for her hunger.

She found herself reaching up a few times to touch the mark Kesh had left, like a pendant one might fidget with. One time, Kesh caught her doing it, and Irina could have sworn she heard the alien mumble something under her breath that sounded like, "Mine." If that was what she said, she had the right of it.

After all, she had been lusting after Kesh for so long, but the months of talking and learning about each other solidified Irina's respect for Kesh. Irina had always needed to respect anyone she dated—it was her biggest turn-on—and she had never respected anyone more.

They had a tasting to get through first though. She handed Kesh a spoon and indicated for her to try it even as she scooped some into her own mouth. Irina rejoiced at the expression on her beloved, scarred face and knew that it matched her own. Rapture.

Around her mouthful, Kesh, lavender eyes glowing, exclaimed, "Goddess, that is divine." A note of something else entered her eyes then, that Irina had only a moment to wonder at. Just as she had been coming out of her foggy brain, she was heading right back into it. Kesh moved fast. Even as Irina registered the clink of Kesh's spoon hitting her plate, she found herself thoroughly kissed. Deeply. They both tasted of the sweet blend of their confection.

The air hitting her upper thighs brought her around enough to understand that Kesh had her dress pulled up. The alien stopped the kiss and looked Irina in the eyes, one eyebrow raised in question. Irina didn't have any question of what she wanted though. She reached her hands to join Kesh's and together they had her dress up and over her head. She released it and watched as Kesh carefully laid it on the counter behind them. Irina, once again, found her respect rise for this female. Some would have just thrown it to the ground, but Kesh took the time to care for Irina's garment. She had taken that kind of care all day with Irina too.

Kesh's eyes grew from soft lavender to a fiery purple as her gaze raked Irina's body from top to bottom. "Take off that breast cage. I want to see you." Irina was melting. Much like the forgotten ice cream behind her. Her blood raced through her veins like lava. She did as Kesh demanded and, of course, it felt amazing. Big-breasted girl problems. Trying to go without a bra throughout a busy day, painful, but when you finally get to free those girls at night, it's the best kind of relief.

Kesh's breathing hitched a little, and Irina couldn't help but arch her back a bit, letting her lover get an eyeful of her girls. In fact, she was emboldened to go further. She lifted her hands under her boobs, propping them up, and even giving them a little jiggle. Kesh came closer, she thought for a lick or a touch, but then she reached behind Irina.

Before she knew what Kesh planned, she found her girls drizzled with honey and melted ice cream. "Fuck! That's cold!" The exclamation escaped her lips as she squirmed. The girls were too hot not take offense. It was only a momentary offense, though, because then she felt Kesh's hot mouth licking up the sticky mess off her skin, and Irina could barely stay standing. *Bears don't have weak knees, dammit.*

Kesh must have felt her slow descent toward the ground because she lifted Irina up like she was a mere cub—*damn these aliens are strong*—and sat her on the counter. "Better?"

"Yes. Much."

"Good. I plan to eat all of my dessert with your body as the plate. Now lay back and relax." They were near one end of the worktop, so when Irina laid back—and yelped again as the cold counter encountered her heated flesh—Kesh moved to her side instead of between her legs. Time went by uncounted as each moment filled with infinite pleasure. First it was the honey and ice cream, which found its way to all of Irina's most sensitive places along with Kesh's tongue and lips. Only interrupted as Kesh fed Irina some of the sweet treat before claiming her mouth for a deep, sticky, intoxicating kiss.

She was awash in sensations. Her bear side was basically face in the ground, butt up in the air, and completely impatient. Kesh wasn't done with just the drizzling though. She broke off cookie pieces and placed them all around Irina's body and told her to close her eyes. Irina complied. The anticipation of figuring out where a nip of Kesh's teeth would show up next as she ate the cookie bit driving her wild. A graze of teeth on her nipple. A deep bite at her abdomen. A gentle nibble on the thick part of her thigh.

She was begging before she had decided to do so. "Please, Kesh. Please."

"Please what, Irina mine?"

She loved the sound of that nickname. "Please. I need you. Please make me come."

Kesh moved away, but only to move between Irina's legs. She

felt a tug on her underwear and then coolness as her hot and very wet pussy lips were exposed.

"Wait!"

"What is wrong?"

Irina lifted up on her elbows. "Um. Two things. One. I need you to rinse your mouth please. I don't know how it is for your species, but mine get yeast infections when you mix sugar and private parts. So while I appreciate how much you enjoyed my dessert, I don't want my dessert anywhere near my lower region."

"I had not realized. Of course." She watched as Kesh made her way to a sink and used her hand to cup some water into her mouth, swishing it around, and spitting it out. She repeated the action multiple times and also made sure to wash her face. As she found a towel and dried her face she asked, "And two?"

"I don't know how diseases work between humans and your people. Do you have diseases? Can you get diseases? How does pregnancy work? Here it has to be a male and female partner to make a baby, but that isn't true for all species on this planet. Is that something th—"

"Irina. Relax. Let me answer. Before we approach any planet, we study questions about disease because, of course, we would not want to endanger our people. No. I am not able to get any human sexually transmitted diseases and my people eradicated sexually transmitted diseases in ourselves a while back. So you cannot get anything from me either. Regarding pregnancy, we have developed methods by which two people of any gender can choose to have a baby with some medical help, but for it to happen without intervention, it takes a male and female for the Staraban as well. Do you have any other concerns? I want to make sure you are comfortable before we move on."

"No. I think that covers it."

"Good. Now lay back and let me indulge myself some more."

Irina did as Kesh requested. Her lover lifted first one and then the other of her legs, propping them on Kesh's shoulders. Irina looked down her body when nothing else happened and found

Kesh, head bent, as she appeared to be studying Irina's pussy. "Everything okay down there?"

The warrior gave her a lopsided smile and said, "Just strategizing my plan of attack. Slow and deep, fast and shallow, or maybe even fast and hard? So many ways I want to please and ravage this pussy. It is hard to choose." Kesh's fingers began playing with her pubic hair. Tugging gently and then just running her fingers over it. It was driving her mad.

"Very good. Carry on. Just please don't take too long deciding. I'm dying over here."

"Close your eyes, Irina. I want you to feel me. Block out everything else but my touch."

She took one last, longing look at her golden goddess and closed her eyes again.

The first thing she felt after that was Kesh spreading her lips wide open. The next? Tongue. Wet. Hot. First slow, but then insistent. Greedy. On her labia. Then her clit. Circling her opening. Then back to press on her clit. Then faster and harder. She felt all of those things to her core. It was not going to take long to come like this. "Yes. That feels so fucking good."

In response, she felt one finger breach her opening and then two. Apparently, Kesh had decided on the fast and hard. Irina was not going to last. Her back arched as her insides coiled like a spring deep in her belly. She was so close. So very close. An arm landed on her pelvis pressing her down, keeping her from squirming or avoiding the pleasure. Kesh curved the fingers inside her and—"Oh, God!"—she pumped them faster right into Irina's g-spot, her tongue and lips still wreaking havoc on her clit. It was getting harder and harder to control her leg placement as she began to quiver.

Irina came apart as her orgasm overtook her. Kesh kept moving, gently now, and licking as Irina was coming. The aftershocks had her twitching and clenching at her alien's fingers. She had never felt anything like that release in her life. Pleasure flowed into every part of her body... her mind... her soul. Her legs had flopped off of Kesh's shoulders at some point and were just dangling over the side of the counter now. "Fuck me."

"I just did, Irina mine."

"Yes. I suppose you did."

"You tasted even better than your dessert." She watched through half-lidded eyes as Kesh brought her come-covered fingers up to her mouth and sucked.

"That's so hot." She grinned. At least, she thought that was what she was doing, but she wasn't fully recovered yet, so who knew? "That was spectacular." Of course, Irina was a baker and the words slipped out, "I'm going to have a lot of cleaning to do."

Kesh's laughter was like music to her. She was finally regaining her wits and realized she wasn't done wanting. Cleaning would have to wait. "I want to taste you now."

"Then get on your knees, love."

That commanding tone sent a lovely shiver up her spine. "Yes, ma'am." Getting off the counter was not exactly graceful, but Kesh didn't seem to care one bit. She just fondled Irina's breasts under the premise of helping her move. Irina didn't think tugging on her nipples counted as helpful. Since it was so painfully enjoyable though, she wasn't about to complain.

As she began to drop to her knees, Kesh was undoing the clasps of her one-piece, tan uniform. She then pulled it down the length of her body until she was nude, golden skin gleaming in the light. Her breasts were on the smaller size with pert golden-tan nipples and Irina looked forward to playing with them, licking them, seeing just how hard she could make those peaks. Between her legs, Kesh had no hair. From all she had seen, the aliens had hairless bodies for the most part. *That would sure save a lot on shaving supplies.* Kesh was also muscular everywhere. Lean and toned with six-pack abs, firm thighs, and she bet, if her alien were to turn around, a juicy, biteable butt.

"You must train a lot. So many muscles I want to lick."

"And you will, but not right now. And yes, we train constantly."

"Beautiful."

"As are you, Irina."

"Let me pleasure you."

Kesh stepped toward her and as her pussy lined up with Irina's lips, she braced one hand on the counter behind Irina, one hand went to the back of her head, and she slung one leg over Irina's shoulder. Irina was trapped between the counter behind her and Kesh's pussy in front of her. Heaven. The arousal she had smelled from Kesh was so intense right then, its source less than an inch before her nose.

"Put your hands behind your back, and do not move them. You only get to use your mouth this time. Fuck me with that strong tongue of yours, Irina. Suck me. Make me come."

Irina didn't hesitate. She brought her hands together behind her back and dove right in. She tasted mana. She licked and sucked at Kesh's hard clit as dirty words and exclamations spilled from the warrior's lips, some in the alien language. Kesh yanked on her hair, pulling her head back so Irina looked up at her, and she said, "Fuck me, now." She had not seen Kesh's expression ever go this stern before. She was usually so light and happy, but this expression said, "Do as I say, or your ass is grass."

Irina loved it. She loved the shift in Kesh between her daily self and her bedroom self. It was like Irina was getting a part of her that no one else would see. She wanted it all. So she leaned forward and drove her tongue straight up into her vagina. She was rewarded with Kesh's grip tightening on the back of her head, pressing her fully flush with her vagina, as well as her hips gyrating on her face.

Yes! Fuck my face! That is so damn sexy.

She let her tongue delve deep in and out of Kesh's cunt, and she felt motion near her face. Kesh had let go of the counter and was rubbing her clit while fucking Irina's face. It was the most erotic thing she had ever seen. When she came, Irina heard both of the warrior's hearts stutter, then Kesh moaned gutturally, and cream filled her mouth. She swallowed it down like it was one of her desserts. Not to be squandered.

Kesh dropped her leg from Irina's shoulder, plopped surprisingly graceless to the ground next to Irina, and again, with surprising strength, gathered Irina's body into hers for a cuddle. They sat there wrapped up in each other, relishing the afterglow. "You are out of this world."

It took Kesh only a moment to catch on to Irina's joke, and then they both laughed.

"So are you, Irina mine."

"I like you calling me that. Am I yours, then? Are you mine?"

"Yes. I hope so. I have adored you from afar for too long. I have lusted for you even longer, but I have been truly falling for you for at least a month now."

"I feel the same way. I think…Well, I think I realized the depth of my feelings the day we talked about your family, my family, and basically all the things, and you told me about your dreams and why you decided to work for the Alien Relocation Cooperative."

"Yes. That was an exceptional day for me too. I am glad I am not alone in my feelings for you."

"Same. I can't believe it's taken us this long to acknowledge it. So much wasted time." She didn't want to think about the possibility of relocation just then, so she pushed all thoughts of it away and said instead, "Anyway… As much as I'm enjoying being all up in our feelings, I really can't overlook how messy we made my kitchen. I *have* to clean it, *now*."

Kesh laughed. "I will help you."

Together, they did just that. Scrubbing and sanitizing everywhere. When they finished, Irina set everything ready for the next day. They moved toward the front door and Kesh gave Irina one of her pirate smirks and said, "You were right, by the way. There is no replicating the baking experience in an FDA," with a chuckle.

"Nope. Not a chance." She unlocked the door, and they stepped outside. Kesh grabbed her up into a kiss, which heated her despite the cool evening air. When they broke apart, a light from inside caught her attention. "Oh. I forgot a light. Hang here for a second. I'll be right back."

When she came back to the door, the sight that greeted her flamed her blood for all the wrong reasons.

[6]

TOGETHER

Irina's Bear-y Good Jewish Recipes Cookbook

Notes on distribution:

Contact shifter bookshop owners to see if they'll carry it.

Upload to Monsterzon because you have to.

See if Rakel Rae will hype it up. That bobcat owes you one.

Contact all the Jewish community centers because obviously…

Come back to this list when you figure out if any of it still exists or if you've been relocated. Maybe the aliens would let you advertise in their next round of pamphlets. Check with that hot alien that keeps coming into the shop when you finish.

Always serve with love,
Irina

CHAPTER 6

Redwood City, CA
September 2025

Kesh was a Staraban warrior. She was trained to seek peace, but
when peace was not achievable, she was trained to subdue any
opponent that got in her way. What was not as easy was subduing a
group of opponents. Three or four humans and she would still think
she had a fighting chance, but seven? She also did not want her
sweet baker to get hurt. What did she know of fighting? They could
really hurt her.

She still had not come up with a solid plan to move them away
from the shop when Irina returned. Kesh yelled, "Irina, go back into
the café!"

"What the hell is going on here?" She did not go back into the
café.

Kesh was beginning to lose her focus in her concern for her
lover's safety. "Irina, go back in. It is not safe for you out here." The
attackers were moving to surround them.

"And it's safe for you?" Irina shouted back at her.

"I'm a warrior."

One of the attackers yelled, "It's not safe for either of you bitches."

Irina's response was, "Uh huh," which left Kesh fully exasperated. Her baker kept ignoring her and yelled at the men and women surrounding them. "I repeat. What the hell is going on here?"

One of the women sneered and said, "We saw you kissing this alien"—she spit after the word alien like it left a bad taste in her mouth—"a minute ago. You are a traitor to your species."

"What business is it of yours who the fuck I kiss?"

"We don't like humans who sell their own people out to the invaders. MAD is here to eradicate all the aliens and those complicit with them."

"MAD?"

"Make Aliens Dead. You must have heard of us."

"Nope. And I don't really give a fuck. Run along before you get hurt."

Kesh had heard enough. "I have heard of this militia group that we have been trying to neutralize and they are dangerous. Would you please stop antagonizing the bad humans and go inside the café? This is not a joke, Irina. They could hurt you."

She thought she heard a snort from her baker. Was there something she was missing?

"What exactly about me, a Jewish immigrant lesbian, makes you think that I'm okay with discriminating against a peaceful group, be they aliens or locals, because some douchebags tell me to?"

A few of the militia pulled out something metal from their coat pockets. They flicked their wrists releasing a hidden blade. Kesh was now truly frightened for Irina. She reached out and tried to grab her arm, but at the same time chaos erupted.

A couple of the men and a woman began to approach Irina while at the last moment, Kesh sensed one was coming up right behind her. She spun in time to bring up her arm, blocking his which had a blade in it. With a few swift moves, she had him unconscious on the ground and his blade in her hand.

When she spun back to Irina, she had moved farther away from

Kesh and many of the militia were focused on her. *No!* She had to find a way to save her. Why was Irina looking so calm?

Irina then spoke, "This is your last warning, guys. And, Kesh, I was just about to tell you about this when these jackasses showed up."

"Tell me about what?"

One guy lunged, and Irina evaded by jumping to one side. But she was not there long. In fact, suddenly she was not there at all. Instead, a giant brown animal—no, not just any animal, a giant brown bear—stood where Irina had been. Kesh looked back up at the sign over the café and could not help herself from laughing.

Her lover was full of surprises.

As her fear was replaced with humor, Kesh relaxed. She was going to join in the fight, but as she watched, some of the men and women ran screaming, some began begging for their lives, and of those still attacking, well, it was not even a little fight. One swipe of Irina's giant claws and the begging attackers begged harder as their friends fell down screaming.

One minute there was a bear, and the next, Irina was back and talking to the begging men. "I suggest you grab your wounded friends and take them to a hospital. I would also suggest that you never speak about what you saw me do, or I might choose to hunt you down for lunch. Lastly, and it goes without saying but I'll say it anyway so we are clear: Never return here. If I see or smell you— remember, I have a bear's sense of smell—I won't be so generous. Make sure to tell your runaway friends those rules too so I don't have to eat any of them for lunch one day."

Kesh may have been trained for peace, but she found Irina's savagery arousing. All of that power and she submitted to Kesh's demands willingly. If she had not loved the baker before, she definitely did now. As the militia fled, carrying their fallen, Irina wandered back toward Kesh with a weary look in her eyes.

Irina spoke as she drew close. "So. Yeah. Surprise. I'm a bear shifter."

"I saw that. Come here."

"Okay." She stepped closer wearily.

Kesh wrapped her arms around Irina's shoulders, pulling her tight. The baker's stiffness slowly melted away, and she put her arms around Kesh's waist.

"You're not mad? Or scared? Or disgusted?"

"No, Irina mine. I have dealt with many species. You should see the Eusart. Very stick like. I *am* surprised since we did not know of humans like you."

"That is because humans don't know we exist."

"Then it makes sense we did not know. But, I am not scared or disgusted. In fact, I am relieved that you are okay. I am also very turned on. I love that you can defend yourself. That you are not fragile. That you give me all of your powerful self. Thank you for being mine."

Irina squeezed a little too tight, but it lasted only a second so Kesh just held her breath until she was released. Then she cupped Irina's beloved face and kissed her. This time, she took her time, worshipping Irina's lips, her cheeks, her whole face.

When they pulled apart, Irina said, "Will you come home with me? I want to learn what else you've wanted to do to my pussy."

"Yes. I was hoping you would ask. Are you opposed to, I think you call it, fisting, here on Earth?"

Irina smiled wickedly, "Most definitely not opposed."

"Good."

Hours later as they lay contentedly in Irina's bed, Kesh was just about to fall asleep, memories of her hand gliding in and out of Irina's slick pussy keeping a smile on her face as she did, when Irina whispered to her.

"Kesh?"

"Yes?"

"Would you want to come with me to celebrate Rosh Hashanah with my family? If it's not too soon or too weird or anything."

"I would enjoy that very much. Thank you."

"You say that now, but wait until you meet them all. So many bears in one place becomes a madhouse."

[7]

PARTY

Irina's Bear-y Good Jewish Recipes Cookbook

Notes on dedication:

I would like to dedicate this book to my family, to my heritage, to my clan, and to my roots. Mostly I want to thank my Babushka for all of her stories. This book wouldn't exist without your fearless baking.

That seems a bit lame. Come back and tweak it. You shouldn't mention the clan. What are we, *Clan of the Cave Bear*? LOL I'm such a dork. Fix it.

Always serve with love,
Irina

CHAPTER 7

Redwood City, CA
September 2025

The last couple of weeks had been the best weeks of Irina's life. Kesh had slept over almost every night, and when she didn't, Irina slept on the Staraban base with her. They had agreed to keep her shifting between the two of them. Kesh understood her family's desire to keep their secret. As long as it didn't endanger anyone, she agreed to stay silent. All had been going so well, but tonight she was a jumble of nerves.

It was one thing to accept the bear you cared for, it was a whole other thing to be surrounded by a clan of them. Hell, even she thought they were a lot to handle sometimes. They parked near the wooded area where her family lived when in the wild, near Muir woods, and walked the rest of the way to the clearing.

Her mother must have been keeping a watch for them, since Irina had told her she was bringing her girlfriend with her, because she spotted them right away and made her way over. *Oh boy. Here we go.* "Hello, Mama. Let me introduce you to Kesh. Kesh, this is Mila Rivkin."

Irina had warned Kesh, and apparently rightly so, about bear hugs. Kesh hadn't raised any objections to them, so Irina hadn't bothered to warn her family off from whatever came naturally. And naturally, the tall warrior found herself ensconced in a giant hug from Mila who welcomed her to the family. Kesh seemed to take that okay. Irina knew it wouldn't last. Poor warrior. So stoic in the face of such a massive attack. Irina's aunts and uncles and cousins and nieces and nephews and forty hugs later, Kesh looked worse for wear. Irina tried to hide her amusement but must have failed.

Kesh leaned over and whispered in her ear, "I see you laughing at me, little baker, and I will get my revenge later for this." Kesh stood in surprise as she heard people around them break out laughing. She looked to Irina for an explanation.

Irina raised an eyebrow in amusement, "Apparently my lesson on bear hearing didn't take, warrior."

Irina had never seen Kesh blush before, but her golden skin definitely took on a darker hue around her cheek area. She recovered quickly though and rejoined, "Apparently we are both due more lessons."

More laughter broke out amongst her family and her mom walked up again, "I like this one. You keep her."

"Yes, Mama."

"Now go introduce her to your papa and your babushka. Your father and grandmother have been patient while all these other ridiculous bears jumped in."

"Yes, Mama. Just point me in the right direction. Also, could you send some of the young pups to grab my baked goods from my car?"

"Yes. Consider it done."

They walked over to the sitting area and found her papa and babushka sitting together. Irina loved her father. He was a tree of a man, and a total teddy bear with his family. As soon as he saw her, he stood up with his arms outstretched. Irina jumped into his arms yelling, "Papa!" and got the tight hug she always wanted from him. She squeaked, which was his indication to put her back down.

After, she leaned down and hugged and kissed her beloved

babushka. She was the one who first taught Irina to bake and those times together in the kitchen were some of her favorite moments from her childhood.

"Papa… Babushka… I would like to introduce you to Kes—"

She didn't even get her beloved's name out before her father had Kesh in a giant hug. "Papa!"

It sounded like Kesh was trying to say something, but Irina knew firsthand that during her papa's bear hugs, air was something quite lacking. Kesh finally squeaked and was swiftly returned to the ground heaving air. "Was he trying to kill me?"

Kesh tried to play it off as a joke, but Irina heard the real inquiry below the surface and shrugged like, "What ya gonna do?" What she said though was simply, "Bears."

She did finish the introductions and her babushka, Leah, instantly grabbed Kesh's hand to study her palm. Kesh looked at Irina with alarm. Or maybe curiosity. "Palm reading is a family tradition from long ago, from before our migration from the Russian Empire."

Kesh got a pat on the hand and a nod from Leah, who turned to Irina and said simply, "Good job." Then she turned back to Kesh and said, "Welcome to the family."

Irina loved her family, but seriously, it had only been two weeks. They hadn't even fully said the "L" word nor done the biting ceremony or anything. Outwardly, to put Kesh at ease she rolled her eyes. Inwardly, she was joyous because having Kesh be a part of her family was all she could hope for.

There was no doubt in her head or heart that she was completely in love with her alien and that she wanted to be mated to her. She thought Kesh might feel the same, but they just hadn't quite crossed that line. Still looming was relocation. What would happen when it was her area's turn? Mountain View, which wasn't far away from where she lived, had already been relocated. Tonight was not a night for dwelling on that though, so she pushed those thoughts aside once again.

She led her lover away from the crowd to check in. "How are

you doing after"—she waved her hand in the general direction of the clearing—"all that?"

"You were not kidding about the hugging. It is not what I am used to, but actually not that far different. My family is also very warm with those who they embrace as family."

"That isn't weirding you out? That they keep welcoming you. I mean, we haven't really been together that long and haven't discussed anything long-term yet, and—"

Kesh silenced her with a kiss, putting an end to Irina's nervous ramblings.

When she broke the kiss, Kesh said, "If the multitude of love marks I leave on you, the fact that I call you mine, or the fact I do not like to be parted from you for long has not made it clear, I want long-term with you. I love you. I do not ever want to give you up. If I have to move to New Earth with you, then I will."

"I love you too. So much, moye zolotse." Relief oozed like melted caramel through her veins. "You really are my sun. One look from you and I am warm all over. You know...I could come live with you if you needed me to. I want long-term as well. As long as possible."

"Then stop worrying and kiss me again before we have to return to your family."

Irina gently pressed her lips to Kesh's, sucking at her plump lower one, loving every breath, every taste she captured from them. She abruptly stopped as she realized they weren't alone. She looked down to find three bear cubs staring up at them. Kesh followed her gaze and, well, Irina had seen the warrior in many ways—stoic, happy, friendly, demanding, sensual, and many more—but she had not seen her like this.

Kesh kneeled close to the ground, looking the cubs in their cute little faces, and became a teenager with a fandom. "You are all so cute! Do you hug too? Can I cuddle you?" She could swear that her girlfriend suddenly had emoji heart eyes as she spread her hands out to the bears.

They were bears. They never missed a chance for some wrestling and hugging so they pounced. Kesh was rolling around on the ground with bears jumping over her playfully until they each found a section of her body to snuggle against. Irina looked on with so much affection filling her body that it was hard to keep in.

"You look so tough laying there amongst the pups. Such the mighty warrior."

"I am never leaving your family. If we had not settled it before, this solidifies it." She flashed Irina the biggest smile, and Irina lost the fight with her joy.

This had Kesh looking concerned, so she rushed to assure her, "Happy tears, love."

The smile came back to her scarred face and illuminated her. She practically glowed.

Later, as the festivities were under way, Irina described some of the prayers that they recited, like the Hamotzi over the circular bread called the challah, and their meaning. She explained what the shofar was and even the method by which you blow into the ram horn to produce the unique sound. She explained about tossing the bread down the river known as tashlich, or the casting off of sins.

Unlike when they were baking, Kesh's eyes never grew glassy. This was clearly right up the alien's alley. Kesh asked so many questions and if Irina didn't know the answer, she sent her to one of the elders.

Wine, vodka, and medovukah were flowing. The food was in abundance. Kesh leaned over and a bit goofily said, "I love everything about you. First there is you. Then, your lovely if a bit lacking in personal space family. And now, sharing with me your traditions. Oh…and bear cubs! I cannot forget the bear cubs."

"Oh, yes, we should never forget about the cubs. I love you too, Kesh. I look forward to learning all about your family and traditions as well."

"Want to know one tradition that I have now?"

"What's that?"

"I have decided that every Rosh Hashanah, being the new year and all, is now a try-something-new-together after-party."

"I don't think that is quite in line with the traditional meaning of the holiday per se, but I am not super religious nor opposed to adding more ways to celebrate. Love should always be celebrated, after all. What did you have in mind?"

"How do you feel about this thing I read about recently, called pegging?"

Irina clamped a hand over Kesh's mouth as bawdy laughter broke out among her family. She felt as her cheeks flamed hot pink. Kesh, understanding her mistake, buried her head into Irina's shoulder, repeating the words, "What have I done?" to herself.

From the side, Leah spoke loud over all the chattering and said, "Bears never run from a challenge, Irinochka. I suggest you wait until you get home though, milaya moya."

That was how Irina found herself bundled up in her car with Kesh, flying down the highway toward home. Kesh was still hanging her head in mortification. "You know, it might be a bit embarrassing, but we are bears. If you think some of my family hasn't found themselves coupling in the woods from time to time with other family members trying to close their ears, you would be wrong."

"Really? Or are you just trying to make me feel less ashamed?"

"Really."

Kesh seemed to rally after that. "Well, if this is my new normal, super-hearing people around me, then I guess I will learn to embrace the embarrassment. Will you be taking your babushka's advice, Irina mine?"

Irina looked over briefly and found Kesh leering at her. Her panties went instantly wet. That was all it took. One look, and she was a goner. "Are you saying you have the tools needed for such an endeavor?"

"I did happen to pick up one of those strap-on dicks I saw in one of your sex shops while I was looking for a, I think it is called, flogger, to use on my beloved."

Irina was going to drive them off the road. "You got us a flogger?"

"Yes. I even hired a human from the store to teach me how to use it."

"I want all of the above."

"Then it's a good thing I have it in a bag in the back seat."

"In the backseat! What if the cubs had grabbed it while pulling out my baked goods earlier?" Her alarm was clearly mirrored in Kesh's expression. The warrior swiftly reached into the backseat and under Irina's chair and pulled out a bag. Kesh opened it and peered inside and apparently, based off of the sigh of relief coming from her, they were spared at least one embarrassment for the day.

"You know, if I had known you were such a kinky alien months ago when we met, I might have had to jump you straight away."

"If I had known you were a bear who was willing to submit to me in bed, I would have pushed you to your knees then too."

"Of course, then we wouldn't have gotten to know each other the way we have. Dreams, families, and all."

"Agreed. I am glad for the time that brought us together for more than just our desire. Will you answer me a question I have had for some time now?"

"Of course."

"How does your shifting work? I have tried to study shifter things, but each book seems to have some different way that it happens and none of it matches what I have seen with you."

"Yeah. I love a good shifter romance, but it's clear that some shifters out there are mocking humans by giving them a bunch of false information. We are magic based. The backstory is long and I can share it with you another time, but basically, the bear and I are one. We just magically exist in a different dimension and when I shift, I am replacing one of my forms with another of my forms, but both forms are me. It is why anything I have on me before the shift is still there when I return. I'm not actually changing either shape so much as displacing it."

"How fascinating. I would like to hear the origin story some time."

"No problem. I have a shifter storybook I can give you."

"I will look forward to it."

The drive back took some time, and they spent it talking about what they planned to do if Irina's area was marked for relocation and about some of the trouble the Staraban were running into from a group called HARM. Kesh assured Irina that HARM, while a problem, were not like MAD. They weren't actively trying to kill aliens, they just seemed interested in finding a way to make ARC leave. Irina didn't like that idea much better, since it would complicate matters for her and Kesh, but at least Kesh was safe from attacks from another group.

They pulled up to her home and parked; Kesh grabbed the bag as Irina unlocked the front door. Once they were inside, all conversation was a thing of the past. They both ripped into their own clothing. Kesh crashed to the ground having forgotten, in her haste, to take off her boots before her jumpsuit. She ended up bare-assed on the floor laughing. Irina smiled down at her. "Who is kneeling to who now?"

"It is not about who is on the floor, my love; it is about who is in control of the pleasure." She said this as she removed her shoes and pants. "Since you are standing, bring your sweet pussy over to me so I can suck on your clit and get you ready for…more."

"Resistance is truly futile. I'm at your mercy even from above. I can't say no once you pull out that dirty talk."

Kesh brought her to her first orgasm with her mouth within minutes. When Irina's knees betrayed her yet again, Kesh had picked her up, laid her gently on her side on the bed, and then left for a brief moment. Irina was coming back to full awareness as Kesh walked in with the bag. "I prepped and cleaned everything in here. Are you still ready to try some new things, my love?"

"Yes."

"Then turn on your stomach, hands above your head, and your legs spread wide for me."

They had played a lot of kinky games together from restraints to spankings the past couple of weeks and kept a running discussion on what things worked and what things weren't working. So far, Irina had discovered a never before tapped desire for a bite of pain. She had asked Kesh if she was interested in giving her some pain, and they had agreed to work into it slow. So far, everything they'd tried had brought them both pleasure. She was ready for more, so she got into position exactly as Kesh commanded her to.

"I love your soft curves so much. You look lovely laying there waiting for me to do whatever I want. Those curves are mine. Every last one of them."

"Yes. All yours, lubov moya."

She heard as Kesh hit the flogger against what had to be her own flesh. "This will make you feel so good. You will tell me if it becomes too much, yes?"

"Yes. Of course."

"Good."

Thud.

Irina groaned into the bed. It was a gentle, almost massage like hit. It felt wonderful.

"More?"

"Yes, please."

Thud. Thud. Thud.

Kesh continued for a few minutes landing firm, massage-like hits across different parts of her body. Her butt. Her shoulders. Her thighs. Her training was clearly thorough, though Irina'd had no doubt since Kesh struck with perfect precision all the allowed areas and avoided all the danger zones. Irina might have watched some videos about this in the past. It's good to stay informed.

"You look so relaxed."

"I am. It feels amazing."

"Are you ready for a little pain, then?"

"Yes." Irina braced herself for the hit, but only some more gentle thuds landed. She relaxed again.

Thwap.

She gasped as the flogger ends flicked at her ass causing a stinging sensation.

"Was that okay?"

"Yes. It hurt, but…Um…I liked it."

"Good. I enjoyed watching your ass quiver with the impact and then clench and release as you processed the pain." As she spoke, Kesh ran a hand over the cheek she'd hit and then squeezed, driving another gasp out of Irina. "Stay relaxed and I will give you more."

"I will."

Thirty minutes later, Irina was still face down on her mattress, but her knees were bent, with her ass up in the air. Her bear was totally down for this position. She was so turned on after the sensual torture Kesh subjected her to that she just kept repeating, "Please," like some kind of broken record.

Finally, Kesh lined up her body to Irina's and as the warrior's hands slid up Irina's body to cup her breasts, her fun-sized, fake cock slid into Irina's pussy. When it was nearly all the way in, Kesh pinched Irina's breasts and thrust the rest of the way—hard. Irina's body bucked from the layers of pain and pleasure. Their first session with the flogger had left much of her butt and upper back sensitive. Kesh was running her breasts along that part of her back while her hips slammed into her butt and both actions brought on even more pleasurable, torturous pain. "Kesh. I need you so much."

"I know. And I plan to give it all to you. All of me is yours anytime you want it."

Kesh set up a rhythm of slow, deep thrusts followed by sudden swift harder ones. It kept Irina's body on a precipice. Wanting to fall over, but just not quite getting there. "Please. Please, Kesh. I can't. Please."

She felt the cold lube as Kesh rubbed it into her asshole. In her blind passion, she had forgotten all about the ass play, but she was so far gone, she was ready for just about anything that would get her to come. Kesh brought her back to a simmer with gentle, easy glides as she worked one, then two, then three fingers in. It was slow and methodical, and Irina ended up drifting on endorphins and sensations. Even the scent in the room was turned up somehow. A sexual drug all its own. It was so thick now she could taste it, and it tasted of them.

By the time Kesh pulled out of her pussy and brought the now lubed up strap-on to her anus, Irina gladly pushed back. Gladly welcomed the low burn. Gladly invited Kesh to fill her in any way, in all ways. She found no pain in the act. Not with where her head was and with how prepared and gentle Kesh was being.

"Good girl. Now, you get to come."

Relief was its own form of aphrodisiac. Finally. She was wild with wanting and found herself riding back, meeting Kesh thrust for thrust. Kesh grabbed her ass cheeks and massaged the flesh there. "I love this ass so much. I looked at it every chance I had. Did you know that?"

"No. Oh God!" Kesh had punctuated her "No" with a brutal squeeze.

"I did. Watching you as you let me take this ass is so fucking hot. I might come just from this. Take your hand and put it between your legs. Play with your clit. Make yourself come for me, Irina mine."

What else was Irina going to do but obey? It took almost no time at all. A few flicks of her finger, and she went flying into an almost painful but glorious orgasm. She might have screamed. She couldn't be sure. She fell flat on the bed, boneless.

Kesh took off the strap-on and cuddled Irina to her side, kissing her. Then she used another new toy, a vibrator, to bring herself to orgasm all while Irina worshipped her with her mouth, the only thing that seemed to still be working.

"May I bite you?" Irina had been too afraid to ask before tonight, but since they'd committed to a future together, she'd decided it was time.

"You mean like a hickey?"

"No. Hmm…Let me explain more about shifting. While a full shift happens inter-dimensionally, certain aspects of both forms can be called upon when needed. For example, I still think with my human brain while I'm in bear form. While in human form, I can make small changes. I can grow my nails into claws if I need to. I can also extend my canines to be longer, sharper. When we find a mate, or someone we want to consider mating, we begin growing that bond through biting. The more we bite, the stronger the bond and it eventually becomes a permanent link."

"Does it hurt or cause permanent damage?"

"It can hurt momentarily, but not continuously and no lasting damage. I just direct some of my shifter magic into the wound and it heals instantly."

"Then, yes. Please bite me."

Irina leaned over Kesh's neck, extended her teeth and bit down, breaking the skin. Kesh tensed beneath her, but clutched Irina closer.

Irina thought at Kesh, "When we are linked like this, we can communicate without talking."

She heard Kesh's hesitant response in her own head, "You can hear me think at you?"

"Yes."

"You grow ever more amazing, Irina mine."

"This only works while I am biting you to start, but it strengthens as the bond strengthens. Eventually, the mind-link becomes a permanent thing that we will be able to do."

"I am going to look forward to that eventuality. You have my permission to bite me as often as you like."

Irina held on for another few seconds—not wanting the connection to end—but as she pulled away, just as she had told Kesh, she sent some of her magic into her spit and licked the wound closed. Kesh felt her neck in surprise. "You said it was instant, but I guess I assumed it would still take a little bit of time. That is some strong magic."

"Yes. It takes a lot to sustain a person and a bear."

"I guess that would be true."

Irina laid her head on Kesh's chest, listening to the double thumps of her hearts. They stayed wrapped up in each other, drifting on contentment. Finally, Kesh spoke. "Your desserts were a big success with your family."

"Yes. They were. Thank you for helping me make them all."

"It was my pleasure. I want you to know, Irina, how much it meant to me that you included me in your celebration tonight with your family."

"It meant a lot to me that you agreed to come."

"Who knew I would meet my *braif* lightyears away from home on an unknown planet?"

"What does *braif* mean?"

"I think the equivalent on Earth is fiancée, which I realize is not exactly what we are, but I have a feeling it is where we are going."

"In Yiddish, we have a very similar sounding word—bashert. It means destiny or soulmate. You are *my* bashert."

Kesh leaned in, kissing Irina's temple, "Happy New Year, Irina mine."

"Rosh Hashanah Sameach, Kesh. To a new year together."

"And to all the new years to come." Kesh thought for a moment, smiled her pirate smile, and said, "Where do you keep your honey?"

Irina had the feeling that their love was always going to be just a little bit messy. She was fine with that…mostly. *Well, bear-ly.* Her pun amused Irina so much, she was smiling when Kesh walked back in.

"I will make it my personal goal to give you a reason to show me that smile at least once a day."

That was when Irina noticed the giant bowl of various foods Kesh had in her hand. "Oh no you don't! We have reached my limit!" She jumped up, rather spry for a bear, and took off running, streaking the house in laughter.

From behind her she heard, "Have I told you how much I love your ass?"

Hours later, after many shenanigans and then clean up, they once again found themselves in bed. With newly changed sheets because despite her attempt at escape, Kesh eventually had her bedroom buffet feast which included a very traditional apples dipped in honey, served in a very nontraditional method, the honey in Irina's belly button.

Now came the best part, though. The part she lived for. Lying in each other's embrace. Holding Kesh close, listening to her heartbeats, and knowing no matter where they ended up, she was home.

Redwood City, CA
October 2025

Irina opened her email to find something from Kesh. Would she be flirting? Commanding? Enquiring? She loved receiving mail from her alien. It always brightened up her day so she quickly opened it.

To: Irina
From Kesh
Subject: Big News

Relocation is on hold. I cannot go into the details of why right now, but I had to tell you. We do not have to worry about where you will be in the future because, for now, we are staying on Earth and relocation has become optional.

· · ·

There has been so much going on around the base that I am only now learning about. Not exactly true. I knew we had a HARM prisoner at one point and about an escape attempt, but there is so much more to tell. Not that anything would have torn us apart, I would not have let it, but this makes me so happy. We have dinner with your family in the sukkah tonight for Sukkot so I can explain it to everyone at once and then you and I will have some celebrating to do.

Love you, Irina mine.
Your Kesh

MOVING JACK EXCERPT

PROLOGUE: JACK THE BLOGGER

Adventures of a Supernatural Geek Girl
April 8, 2020

Dear Reader,

Coming to you straight from the heart of Silicon Valley. First entries can be so challenging. What can I write to break the ice and get people reading my blog? And how... when... do I mention I'm a vampire? Do I just throw it out there, have an interesting lead in, hint at it but don't come right out and say it? Or talk around it until it's a dead fish and move on?

Now that I've sautéed that sucker, let's get this blog on a roll.

Since I've mentioned it, I'm sure you've got some questions. So did I! I was killed two months ago, accidentally killed my maker, came back to life, and had to figure out vampirism all by my lonesome. My questions started with, "What the fuck? Why am I so hungry? Am I really a vampire now? What the fuck?" Once I got past that newbie-in-shock awkward stage, my questions were, "Who am I now? What can kill me? Am I the undead, the walking dead, the glittery kind, the altered-DNA kind, or something else entirely? Do I have to drink blood and if so, how much and from what source? Is there a *Vampire for Dummies* I can download? Really though, WHAT THE FUCK?"

Luckily, I had the means to find answers. You see, I'm also a hacker. I scoured the internet for true knowledge instead of myths. Myths get you killed. Eventually, I ran across a well-hidden book. At first, I was sure it was a work of fiction. It contained a vampire origin story and a set of rules. The snarky sounding rules made me think I was looking at myth but since I enjoy good snark, I chose to test them out anyway. Goldmine! Hence, I'm still here.

You may ask yourself, why would a vampire start a blog? Good question. You see, I was bad with social situations before I became a vampire. Now I'm a walking double whammy of social dysfunction. I'm hoping with this blog I can bring other vampires useful information and, in the meantime, form a community. Isn't it ironic as a science and tech buff I always believed in aliens and not the things that go bump in the night and yet, here I am... Never did meet an alien. So. Here's your first vampire...

Fun Facts:

Vampires are all environmentalists. Who knew? Right? This is because we're intimately connected to the Earth. Goes back to that origin story I mentioned before. I was always environmentally concerned, because you're just being a douche if you don't care at all, but as a vampire I'm a total bitch when it comes to mother Earth. If I see you don't recycle something, I may just go fang on your ass. Not really, but #TakeCareOfOurMother.

Hugs and bites! iByte

---

[1] - SEE JACK RUN

Adventures of a Supernatural Geek Girl

September 30, 2025

Dear Reader,

Over the last five and a half years of blog entries, an alien invasion, and the rise of the resistance, I feel like we've really gotten to know each other. Lately, some of you have brought it to my attention that I never discuss my dating life. I'd think with the aliens' relocation plans looming, you'd have more important things to think about, but apparently I'd be wrong.

I would *like* to say I don't discuss it because I'm busy being a rebel. ¡Viva la revolución! I would *like* to say it's because I'm too busy with an overly full dating life. I almost choked on writing that. I would also *like* to say it's because a lady never kisses and tells but this vampire would totally kiss and tell. You see, dear followers, before I can report said kisses, said kisses would have to happen. <sigh>

In my pre-vampire imaginings of vampires, they were all sexy and having sex all the time. Dating gods! Am I right? When I became one, I kinda assumed, it was like a fairy godmother waving her wand and making me the ultra-datable. Turns out, you can make the girl a vampire but you can't teach her to flirt, or dress, or be less awkward. I still get along better with my computer than with the general population. I can help lead a resistance but don't ask me to hold a conversation with a guy I'm interested in.

Don't get me wrong, I'm not completely innocent. I'm a vampire, not a zombie, not that I'm saying those exist. Moving on. Let's just say my dating life has been nothing to write home about and few and far between.

I've come to accept that I'm not the kind of girl who has guys chasing after her. If anything ever changes, you'll be the first to know .

Flashback Fun Facts:

Vampires can be out in the sunlight, just not for prolonged exposures. We have an internal turkey popper that tells us when we're nearing our exposure limit. I could be sitting right next to you at the beach. (Just not for too long. That could get messy.)

Hugs and bites! iByte

<hr>

Redwood Grove, Los Altos, CA, USA, Earth
October 1, 2025

Jack Daniels nervously looked up from her wrist phone, tapped the implant in her ear, and whispered, "Hal, off." Hal was her personal assistant link (PAL). The PAL program had been her baby before the aliens had arrived. Now, her baby was at a standstill, and she had one of the few PALs left in existence. It was thoroughly disheartening to think she'd just been using Hal to scroll through the latest comments posted to her blog entry. What a waste of a good PAL. Still, Hal definitely made it easier to multitask and keep up with her readers.

She'd been in the middle of getting offended that one commenter offered to date her in exchange for immortality—the nerve of some people—when she heard figures approaching her location, and went radio silent. She stood stock still in the clearing off of one of the beautiful Redwood Grove hiking trails. She wasn't sure why the aliens had stuck a terminal out here except maybe they liked nature. Or maybe the location was to calm the humans as they registered for relocation? After all, who could be unhappy surrounded by tall trees, deer, and the sound of water? The answer to that last question is, she could, because she couldn't afford to be caught by the wrong people and especially not by the aliens.

Whoever was approaching, was still some distance away, and she couldn't tell yet, how many were approaching, but her multitasking time was up. Hal testily, but neurologically, answered her, "You could be nicer when turning me off, you know. Rude, much?" She detected a huff from him before he shut himself down, but couldn't remember when she programmed a neurological huff into his code.

At least once out of every two interactions with Hal, she found herself reconsidering the PAL personality profile. That is, if she was ever able to return to working on it. Not any time soon, with how things were going.

Focus!

"Come on. Come on. Come on. Download faster." She anxiously whispered at the aliens' computer terminal, keeping her other senses trained around her. She had zero intention of getting caught.

Ugh, you're talking to inanimate objects again, Jack. Isn't it bad enough you talk to yourself a lot? You know... like you're doing right now? Maybe she needed to spend more time with her friends when she got back to base. At least she still had her sense of humor.

The sound through the trees grew progressively louder, closer. A human would even be able to hear something soon. Anxiety clawed through her, making her feel like a heart attack was imminent, but that was impossible seeing as her heart no longer pumped blood and hadn't for over five years. Not since becoming a vampire. Instead, when anxious or excited, she experienced an energy elevation that made her body thrum and tingle. And boy, was she thrumming and tingling now.

The smart thing to do was to listen to the feeling and take action. Yeah. That was unlikely. She was pretty sure she didn't have a functioning survival instinct.

Since making the right choice was off the table, she continued to stand around waiting for the download to finish. Tapping her foot. Gnawing her lip. She was likely to get herself caught, and with her luck, this particular terminal would only connect her to Staraban recipes and gardening tips. Of course, if the aliens had their way, those things might just prove useful. So yeah.

The Staraban had arrived on Earth eight months earlier freaking all the humans the fuck out, even with their peacenik approach. "We come in peace and are here to save you."

They even came bearing pamphlets. Who knew first contact would involve a freaking pamphlet? In said pamphlet, they claimed Earth was a dying planet and humans were getting relocated to a shiny new habitable alternative. Right! Who believed that? As far as Jack was concerned, when something sounds too good to be true, you shove it right back into outer space.

Focusing back on the task at hand, she was quite sure she was stuck with the slowest computer in the galaxy. She had excellent hacker skills but even she couldn't change the speed of the alien processor. Apparently, the aliens could travel through space but couldn't figure out how to make a computer download quicker than a turtle's speed. *Ladies and gentlemen, this is the insurmountable issue for all sentient beings. Space travel, no big deal. Lasers for weapons, sure. Food replicators, yep. A faster operating system, nope. Sheesh! Who knew?*

Her vampiric senses went on full alert as she picked up more information about the approaching parties. She could now tell that there were two teams of aliens and they seemed unaware of her presence, since they weren't covering their approach nor running at her. It'd be hard for them to pick up her presence anyway, for now, since as a vampire, she didn't need to breathe and didn't have a heartbeat, so she easily kept under the radar. Vampire perks. Of course, if she was still here when they made it to the clearing, she'd be pretty hard to miss.

Still listening for any sign of alarm, all she heard was slow gait, easy breathing, and relaxed conversation. She guessed they were here on pleasure not business and definitely, luckily, were still unaware of her. Since Staraban physiology included having two hearts, she could also deduce that two aliens were approaching from the south, since she caught four heartbeats, and three aliens were approaching from the east, with six heartbeats. If they stuck to their current pace, she calculated that they'd reach her location in about two minutes.

If they'd been human, she could have taken all five of them in a fight, but the Staraban were strong and fierce warriors. She hadn't had to battle with them, yet, but she had seen news coverage of them quelling some of the riots that occurred when humans first learned they weren't alone in the universe. One Staraban in a fight, would be a challenge, though she still thought she could win, but all five, no way. *Come on, Jack! Get this show on the road already!*

Another minute passed, her anxiety clawed even deeper into her, and the computer finally, *finally*, finished downloading the information she needed. Since no one was around to see her do her vampire thing, she moved at a blurring speed, grabbed her drive, shut down the terminal and kept blurring into the tree line to the northwest. *Yep. That's me. Captain Blur. Like the Flash, but not.* She silently chuckled. At least she could amuse herself before getting caught.

She began heading directly back to the Humans Against Relocation Movement (HARM) HQ, but her lack of survival instinct reared its head again. *Who needs sound decision making anyway?* She paused, gauged her distance, and jumped into a tall tree about a quarter mile away. Curiosity may have killed the cat, but the vampire? *Nah. Observation is a form of information gathering, which is why I'm here. Right?*

Jack stopped her imitated breathing as the aliens entered the clearing. It always amazed her just how similar they were in form to humans. In fact, they could sing along to "Head, Shoulders, Knees, and Toes" if they were so inclined. She silently giggled at that thought, picturing the mighty warrior aliens participating in the silly children's song. *Still amusing myself.*

What wasn't the same, besides the whole two heart thing, was that the aliens were also taller and more muscular than most humans. The four males and one female in the clearing were prime examples of this. Jack was five-foot-eight and yet, the aliens were much taller. The males all looked like extras from the movie *300*. Ripped and ready to fight. *I bet they all have a six pack. Or maybe even an eight pack?* The alien female was sleeker but still muscular and tall. Their skin also had a marked golden look to it. Not tan exactly, but not yellow either. It was definitely distinct.

She was loath to admit it, but secretly, she had always found something alluring about them. Jack knew better than to be deceived by their beauty, though. As a vampire, she had run across her fair share of both friendly and cruel vampires and yet they were all beautiful. Well... maybe not her, but all the other vampires. Still, something always drew her to the Staraban. Perhaps because they were such an enigma and she'd never met a puzzle she didn't have to solve.

As far as she could tell, they weren't the Borg nor the Empire. They didn't opt for assimilation or destruction, but instead they seemed to always look for a peaceful solution before going for the beat down. They *seemed* to actually believe they were helping the poor, idiot Earthlings who couldn't be trusted with big decisions like where to live.

She found it hard to remain unmoved while observing their friendly and affectionate demeanor with each other. It was obvious that they were all close. *Friends? Family? Lovers? Do they take more than one lover? How do they even make love? Why the hell am I thinking about this?*

She wished she could hate them. It would make this rebellion so much simpler. Instead of being that boyfriend you *know* is an asshole, they behaved like the irritating one who was generally a good guy but thought you needed his mansplaining to get you through life. *Yeah, right. No man or alien is going to tell me what to do!*

It took her a bit, but she suddenly realized her gaze kept returning back to one specific alien. There was something about him that kept her *riveted.* He had wavy black hair that hung loosely around his head. She couldn't discern his eye color at this distance, but there was an intensity of purpose, an awareness of his surroundings that set him apart. He seemed a man with intense control. Of himself? Of others? Maybe. He just didn't seem as relaxed as those around him. He wasn't classically handsome, though thinking that about an alien was ridiculous anyway, but still, his features were severe with a firm jaw line, wide nose, and slanting brows. No softness that she could tell. A shiver of awareness ran down her back. It was cold, or something. He looked absolutely scrumptious in the alien one piece, form fitting, tan uniform which hugged him like a glove, much like Jack suddenly wished to be doing. *Oh Shit!* Her growing arousal as she stared at him, tripped her vampire switch and her fangs elongated. Blood-hunger and sexual hunger often triggered the same physiological reactions.

She tried to get a grip on her libido. *They're probably just like that TV show V, the original one, not the new one, where it's all good on the outside but you unzip them and, wham, behind door number one is a lizard man!* Unfortunately, desire continued to course through her. As Jack's hunger flooded her veins and pooled in her core, she pictured leading him away and having her way wi—

She tensed. Instinct made her go completely and utterly still.

Tarc wandered into the clearing with his brother, best friend, and second in command, Bren, at his side. He enjoyed every moment he could spend out in nature and took every opportunity to get away from base to do just that. It saddened him to think that Earth, which was a truly beautiful and naturally diverse planet, was dying. For this outing, he and Bren planned to meet up with their youngest brother, Drei, who was set to leave Earth that evening, their beautiful sister, Caran, and their close family friend since childhood and head of security, Nial. They had chosen a stunning wooded area near an outpost they had set up a few months back when they had relocated the humans around it.

"This area is quite lovely." Caran, scientifically brilliant since she was little, studied the trees nearby. "I will need to grab some samples before we leave the area. I want to further study the flora an—"

"Looks like we have lost your sister already." Nial laughed and slapped Bren on the back.

"Yes. Always a risk when encountering any new plants, flowers, dirt, species... basically anything classified as new and organic is fair game for little sis." Bren teased and winked at Caran.

"Similar to your need to study anything classified as female, compatible, and willing. But of course, your study is rather shallow since it lasts for only a night." Caran countered.

Everyone laughed and Bren shrugged. "It is not my fault the females love me. I do not want to hinder peaceful accords."

Drei, a delegate of the All Alien Alliance, coughed. "Brother, you leave so many angry females behind you, I am surprised you are allowed anywhere near a negotiation."

Bren looked a bit sheepish but with a glint of humor in his eyes.

In classic Bren form, he responded, "I am always up front in what is happening, it is not my fault my charm makes them want more than one night."

Caran groaned. "I know I brought it up, but now I regret it. Could we stop talking about my brother's bedroom exploits?"

Nial gave Caran's nose a brotherly tweak which she swatted away irritably. "Just think of it in scientific terms. A study of the male in his natural habitat."

Caran rolled her eyes. "You would know all about that, too. I would rather study the plants around here." She turned to Drei. "Are you ready for your trip back to the Alliance?"

As the others joked and began checking in about their day, Tarc did not participate. His siblings were often amusing to observe, but he did not often join in with their jokes. He never quite knew how to drop his cloak of control, of being in charge, of being responsible. Right now, though, he had another reason he did not participate. Since walking into the clearing his senses had gone on alert. He had tensed, aware of everything. He could not pinpoint the cause of the unease, but something was not right. Something. Something. As he took another breath, he noticed a distinct scent in the air. He let his inner predator take over and breathed a little more deeply to understand where the scent was coming from. There was an abundance of it near the registration terminal but that was starting to dissipate. What he was not prepared for, was how intoxicating he found the scent. He closed his eyes and let it infuse his system. It appeared the strongest was heading into the tree line to the northwest.

He scanned the trees in that general direction. As he did, he could not shake the effect of the smell nor the sure feeling that they were being observed. Then he saw it. No. He saw her. At this distance, there was no way to be sure the person in the tree was a female, but the scent and his gut told him she was. He watched as the figure went unnaturally still. She must have realized he was staring at her.

He took barely a moment to tell his family and friend that he needed the area searched. That he had reason to believe there may be others around. He sent them to the south, east, and west, while he headed directly towards the figure. He ground his teeth as she dropped down from the tree. He picked up his pace, almost running. The words were out of his mouth before he could think better of them. "Do not run, female! I will not harm you!"

That went about as well as he expected and he cringed as her pace increased. His did too and his inner predator shifted all of his attention to tracking his prey.

An hour later, his inner predator was hissing and biting at the bit. Catching her would have been simple, if he had directed the others to help him, but her smell had been so damn enticing. He had wanted her all to himself. Of course, now that he had chased that same smell for so long, through neighborhoods and shopping districts, it was quickly losing its appeal. That was a lie. It was just as intoxicating. He was just tired of trying to hunt her down. He felt both a grudging respect for and a deep frustration with the female.

One thing was for sure, he needed to find her. Her scent had been near the terminal and he wanted to know why. Also, in theory, he was tracking a human female, but he was not so sure about the human part. Her agility, silent movement, and speed hinted at something *more*. He wanted, no, needed to know for sure. Was there another, more dangerous, species on Earth that they needed to be aware of?

He nearly growled out loud when he saw that she had circled him back to the relocated neighborhood near the park where the chase began. He continued to follow her scent, though, which surprisingly led into the abandoned library. He listened intently. A musty smell permeated the air, but her scent... her scent was now very strong and all around where he stood. His muscles went on full alert, ready for action. *She is here.*

"*Fash!*" The Staraban curse flew out of his mouth as he flew forward. He used the momentum to whirl around. Considering the strength of the hit, he gaped at his would-be attacker. Something did not equate.

Crouched in a battle stance was a woman with pale skin, who looked to be in her mid-twenties, by human years. She was only as tall as his chest with a curvy, sensual body. She was wearing the

Earth clothing black boots, black jeans, and a tight, black shirt with the words "People are Interesting. Books are Better." Her dark brown hair with red stripes weaving throughout was pulled back in a ponytail. Her eyes were the color of one of his new favorite Earth foods, chocolate, and shown with a brilliant fire, and her lips... He could not take his eyes off her lips. He knew he should say something, but before he could think of what, she lunged at him again. *Fast.*

He dodged her attack. *Since when can humans move like that?* "Stop! Now." He demanded. Instead, she attacked him, again. He narrowly avoided her.

"Stop following me." she snarled. "I don't want to hurt you, but I will if you make me."

He snorted.

That was a mistake. His little prey narrowed her eyes at him and attacked ferociously. He blocked a few of her hits, but grunted when one landed squarely on his chest, staggering him back. He fisted his hands. *That actually fashing hurt.* He did *not* want to hurt her and so he maintained his position, "I just want to talk, little human."

"Little? You know what... never mind. I meant what I said. Stop following me and leave me alone. In fact, better yet, get you and all your big alien buddies back on your spaceship and go home like E.T."

He had no idea who this eee tee was but he could not miss that her tone dripped with sarcasm. Irritation flitted up his body. He was not going anywhere. "We are here to help yo—"

"Off of this dying planet," she interrupted in a mocking voice. She put her hand on her hip and in her regular voice, added, "Save it. I don't believe you. Want to try again?"

He glared at her. "Are you questioning our honor? We do not lie. *I*, do not lie."

Her answer? She lunged at him again hitting his chest and knocking him even further back.

Different emotions were fighting for supremacy. Anger that this human female dared to question his honor. Annoyance that she was able to land so many hard blows. Curiosity to figure out what she was. Desire. *Desire? Damn, he was horny.* He had always admired a strong, fearless female. There was no fear in this one. Only fight.

As they squared off with each other, he imagined what it would be like to lift her up in his arms, have her wrap those strong legs around his hips, and drive himself right into all of her power and beauty. He was so hard, his cock was trying to punch a hole through his well-maintained uniform. He saw her sniff the air in confusion. *Do humans do that?* Her gaze veered directly towards his painfully hard member and then slowly, seemingly cataloguing his body parts, back up into his eyes with such heat, a growl escaped him.

That was when she pounced again, pushed him hard in the chest, propelling him backward into the wall. He was about to defend himself, when he realized that this time, she had not jumped away. No. This time she was pressed right up against him, kissing his throat as she started clawing at the clasps on the front of his uniform. Some small part of him warned that this was reckless and not like him, but his body stopped listening to that part when he felt her lips on his skin and her hands on his chest. More insistent was the need to get his hands on her too. Both of their lustful scents were now swirling and combining around them in their own mating ritual. It was like being enclosed in an aphrodisiac.

He threaded his fingers into her hair and yanked her head back for a kiss running his tongue along the seam of her mouth until she opened on a sigh. His tongue delved in, tasting her and sparing with her tongue. There was nothing sweet about this kiss. It was either a fight for supremacy or a race to a mutually pleasurable conclusion, he could not tell which, and he did not care. He was operating on pure instinct. He was pretty sure the same was true for the ball of fury and lust in his arms. And that thought just made him even hotter. Harder.

Her hands fumbled with the fastenings and she growled into his mouth, so he pushed her hands out of the way, and undid them all in a few deft moves. She took over and pushed the material off of his shoulders. She had the material most of the way down his chest when she broke from his mouth and started kissing his neck again. Tarc ran his hands from her hair down the length of her back. He could feel the muscles that ran along her body shifting and tensing as she began to kiss her way down his chest. He was not used to giving up control in these types of situations, but there was no way he was going to stop her right then. "You feel amazing."

Their combined scents utterly engulfed him. She was spicy and rich and sweet and it blended perfectly with his own masculine scent. All of his senses were fully tuned in to her. Smell, touch, beauty, taste, and the sounds she was making deep in her throat. The combination was driving him out of his mind and uncomfortably, out of control. The thought, *she is mine*, was on repeat in his head and he could not understand why. Still, he did not have the capacity to question it at that moment.

She fumbled with the clasps at his waist, and once again, he pushed her hands out of the way, and undid them for her. When he finished, he moved his hands up the front of her body, inch by inch until he cupped her perfectly rounded breasts. They filled his hands completely. He wanted to feel them with no clothes between them, so he pushed her shirt up even while she was tugging his uniform down. He lifted her shirt over her breasts and saw she wore a lacy black Earth undergarment underneath. His fingers teased at her nipples poking at the material and she whimpered. He pushed the material down releasing her breasts and felt the weight of them with his palms. She whimpered again and arched her back. He could not stop feeling her and rubbing his thumb back and forth over her very erect, hard nipples.

Her hands, which had stopped moving while he fondled her, now moved to the front of his uniform and gripped his throbbing member. He grunted. "Yes. Feel me." She pulled away from his hands and once again pushed down on his uniform. This time she got it past his erection and even further pooling at his ankles. She came back up, palmed his hard shaft and kissed her way back up his chest. "Your hand on me feels so, so good." His hands went back to tweaking the hard buds of her nipples and he could not wait to get his mouth on them. He was just about to lean down to do just that, when she planted a kiss on his throat and he felt a sharp pain. *"Fash!"*

Before he could register what had happened, she was gone. Left behind was her apology on the wind and her scent still surrounding him. *What the fash just happened? And damn she moves fast.* He considered chasing her again but since his pants were down around his ankles, he knew she would be long gone by the time he could.

He reached up and felt something wet on his neck. He looked at his fingers and saw blood. Anger vied with unfulfilled lust but ultimately, neither won out. He yanked his pants up and re-clasped everything, doubly frustrated, and wondered how he would find his blood-thirsty vixen. *I cannot believe I fell for her seduction. Was it all just a ruse to get away? Thank the goddess that Bren was not here or else he would torment me endlessly for this.*

She may have drawn first blood, but Tarc planned to capture her, find out what she was doing in the clearing, and then... then he would make sure they finished what they just started. *Only this time, I will be in control and she will be begging for me.* First, he needed to find her.

You can keep reading Moving Jack most everywhere books are sold.

CHASING RORY EXCERPT

PROLOGUE: WORLD OF NEWS TIMES

*****Breaking Earth News*****
World of News Times

We scour the internet so you don't have to.

To all our fellow humans, the following news has come from multiple sources within multiple governments. We have verified and reverified our verifications because this is a big deal and we wanted to be sure before we shared it.

All relocation off of Earth is now optional. You heard us correctly. The Alien Relocation Cooperative leaders, the Staraban; and our favorite mostly-peaceful resistance movement, the Humans Against Relocation Movement, have teamed up to prove whether Earth is really dying. Apparently, that has now come into question.

Sources tell us there is a third party involved, but they don't have any more details than that. Something definitely smells fishy and we will keep you informed with any new developments.

Foremost in our thoughts? What about those who have already been relocated? Will they be able to return?

Stay tuned to WONT for answers as they become available.

Phoenix Bordnow
WONT Senior Writer

[1] - ENCOUNTER AT KNIFE POINT

Captain's Log: Earth date October 9, 2025

The Staraban-alien-dumbass, also known as Bren, has decreed that little ol' human me is to stay put on Earth for my own safety. What this oversized, golden, hotness doesn't understand is that there is only one captain of my life and it sure as hell isn't him.

My newest friend and coconspirator, Jill, and I plan to stowaway aboard his ship if I can't convince him, one way or another, to relent. After all, I've only gotten where I am today because of my wit and cunning. Okay, and maybe my ruthlessness.

Whatever.

Don't judge.

Anyway... Hopefully he can be made to see reason because it's not just his ship I want to board and ride. The next captain's log will be made in space because that is the final frontier.

¡Nos vamos!
Rory out.

Staraban Base, Northern California
October 9, 2025

Bren of the Staraban, fierce warrior and second-in-command of the Alien Relocation Cooperative (ARC), never cowered from anyone. The opposite. With his scarred face and tall muscular stature, he was feared by many across the known universe. Therefore, he had to ask himself how he had ended up in the predicament he was in at that moment. Actually, he knew. Two words. Aurora Espinoza. Ever since he met the diminutive, curvaceous, and sexy human female, nothing made much sense.

Rory with her thick, dark brown, wavy hair that he wanted to feel cascading around him as he held her close. Her big, expressive, yellow-green eyes that he wanted to see glazed in desire. Her warm, light brown skin that he wanted to see flushed and naked against his. Her full sensual mouth that he wanted to see wrapped around his— Bren flinched back to awareness as another knife sailed just past his thigh. The very lips he had imagined doing wicked things were currently yelling profanities at him in two Earth languages, as she continued her rather dangerous form of disagreement.

Rory, a munitions expert, which he had only learned about recently, was proficient with most weapons. He hoped with her perfect aim, she was missing him on purpose. She got really fucking close, though. Without turning to look, he could guess that there was a knife outline of him in his wall. Only *she* would come to have a conversation wielding throwing knives. It was hard to tell if her knives or her words could skewer with more painful impact.

"Rory, you are being unreasonable *and* homicidal." He realized his mistake too late because that was the wrong thing to say. Two more knives embedded in his wall. One had come uncomfortably close to his groin.

"I'm unreasonable? Me? ¡Cabrón!" She seemed to use that word a lot around him. "You haven't seen unreasonable. I'm going to go get something bigger to make my point. Don't move." She threw her last knife and this time it caught the slightest bit of his uniform pant leg, pinning it to the wall with an exclamatory thud. She turned and made her way to the exit.

He pulled his leg, hard, ripping his pant leg, and caught up to her just as she reached the door. He turned her around and pinned her to it with his hands on her shoulders. "I think not. Do I need to ask my brother to lock you up for my safety and yours? This is my decision and I will not endanger you by taking you on this mission. That is final. You do not understand the dangers that exist out in space and you are human."

"What does that mean?"

"It means that your species is very easy to kill."

Her eyes narrowed at him. "I have every right to come on this mission. The All Alien Alliance will be hearing and making judgements about events that were perpetrated against *my* planet. *My* people."

He reluctantly agreed that she had a point. They *had* learned the Vrolans had lied about Earth's dying-planet status. The deception was especially disturbing because they had hired his family's company, ARC, to move the humans to another planet. They needed to be reported to AAA to start an investigation. And, in most cases, a representative of the alien species impacted should be there.

But... They did not want to waste time waiting for the various Earth governments to assign a representative and there was no way he would be bringing her. So... point or not, she was not coming.

She continued to argue her case. "Some of my people should be present for this. *You* are being unreasonable. I can defend myself, as the knives in your wall can attest."

"The fact that I now have you pinned to my door and at my mercy says differently. One wrong mo—" He groaned, his dual hearts beating harder, and her name came out as a plea. "Rory." He laid his forehead down on the top of her head. She was so small. So delicate. She had him completely at her mercy, and she knew it. "What are you doing?"

"I would've thought it was obvious. I could've sworn that I'd heard you had a lot of experience with the opposite sex." She continued to rub her hand slowly up and down his ever growing shaft.

"You heard wrong."

"Did I?"

"I have had a lot of experience with everyone."

"We have that in common then."

His breath caught as she squeezed. Her hand was so small and

yet she applied just the right amount of pressure to drive him wild. He wanted so much more. He wanted to feel her hand on his actual cock with no material separating them.

"Rory. You keep that up, and you will see exactly how much knowledge I have. I will make you feel so good. Let me pleasure you."

"You want to bring me pleasure?" Her voice dripped with sex just like his cock was doing.

"Yes. So much pleasure." His hips pushed forward even more fully into her hand. He moved one hand from her shoulder to cup her cheek and turn her face up to his. She looked him in the eyes with a small smile playing along her lips.

"If you really want to give me pleasure—" She paused and bit her bottom lip drawing his eyes and all of his attention to the spot. He was so riveted, that he almost missed her next words, and then his brain registered what she said. "—then I need your respect. Being respected gives me pleasure. Let me come with you on this mission."

He looked back into her eyes and saw the steel there. The resolve. The pride. And everything came back into focus. She was using sex as a weapon. Seducing him to get her way. He wanted this one human more than he could ever remember wanting anyone else, and all she wanted was to come on his mission. His once over-heated blood turned to ice. "No."

He stepped away from her. One step. Two steps. Three. Until he could breathe. Until he could gather his composure.

"You will *not* be coming. I have a lot of preparations to complete and do not have time for your type of *negotiations*." He saw her flinch and hated himself a bit for hurting her.

"Woooow. On Earth mere months and already catching on to harmful stereotypes. Impressive. I tell you that I want to be respected for the independent woman that I am, treated as an equal, and all you see is a woman manipulating you. Well, fuck you."

He was so angry at the idea that she had just been using his desire for her against him, that he did not process whatever else she had just said. Though, it was hard to miss her parting shot of "Fuck you." Yep. Fuck him. He had a mission to get back to planning and did not have time for her manipulations.

Because if he had the time, he would have to admit it hurt that her seduction only happened for ulterior motives.

Because if he had the time, he would have to admit he had wanted her since the moment they met.

You can keep reading Chasing Rory most everywhere, but it is recommended, though not necessary, to read Moving Jack first.

CLAIMING JILL EXCERPT

Chapter 1 — The Jill Element

Fuck-It-All Diary Entry
October 21, 2025
Dear Diary,

I can't believe I've been talked into doing this, but whatever. My new friend Rory suggested I create you, so here you are. Apparently, she thinks I need to therapize or some shit. She *thinks* I should get my thoughts out somewhere because I've supposedly "been through a lot" lately. Bitch, please. My childhood, now that was a lot.

And, okay, now that it's Nial and I, alone, for the next twelve days on a small spaceship, returning back to Earth, it's possible and even probable that I will need someone to talk to who won't turn every conversation into a screaming match. Fair.

The main reason I feel compelled to get you started though, is to keep a record of all the wild shit that I've learned of lately. I mean, if what I've experiences lately was in the first few weeks of knowing this new group of friends and of life outside of a militia, who knows what might come next?

It all started the day I decided to defect from MAD. That's the militia group I was raised in since dear old dad is the leader, and I hadn't had a mom since I was young.

It's also the same group currently trying to kill all the aliens back on Earth. It's in the freaking name, Make Aliens Dead. Real original, right? Dad's not the most creative with names, but he is when being devious, underhanded, or cruel. Yep, he has all the best qualities in a dad. Did I mention that since my defection, he's issued a command that I be killed on sight? Yeah... Dad of the mother-fucking year.

And, now? Now he's the reason I have to prematurely end my space adventure. There I was, finally having a good time, Rory and I shooting the shit as we stowed away undetected for days on Bren's ship. Getting caught, could have been the end of it, but nope, things somehow had gotten even better. We were training on weapons and learning the fighting techniques of the Staraban. Did I mention that's the name of the aliens? Anyway, it was heaven compared to my upbringing.

Okay, sure, one could say I had a near death experience, so it wasn't all good, but I didn't die and that wasn't the first near-death experience I've had, so all-in-all a positive outcome in my book. I was looking forward to rejoining Rory and the rest of the crew doing space travel, warrior shit.

But noooo... Dear old dad has to go and ruin *this* for me too, threatening death and destruction back on Earth so I felt I had to volunteer to try to fix it. Yeah. So, here we are. I'm now heading back to Earth instead of exploring space. To say I'm angry about it, well, I was already angry at him before this shit. Can't get more angry than wanting to end someone, I figure.

To top all this, I'm heading back with Nial. The alien who angers, challenges, disturbs and fascinates me in equal measures. He volunteered to be my pilot and I had no say in the matter. Not that I know what I would have said if given the option. Did I mention how complicated my feelings were where he's concerned?

Well, I met *him* the day I defected, too, assuming you call getting tackled by an alien, "a meeting."

I just realized I hadn't explained what all has been going down lately. Oops. My bad. I guess you could say the day I defected changed everything.

The rundown goes like this: escaped from the militia by capturing an alien and a fucking vampire. Yes… you heard me, a fucking vampire! I realized they were my ticket out, which becomes a much longer story. Needless to say, I ended up befriending that fucking vampire, Jack, as well as her best friend Rory, who I've mentioned multiple times. That bitch Rory, and I mean that in the best way, turned out to be a shifter because, of course she did. I'm still waiting for my introduction to a zombie and a fairy.

Too much happened to go into, but some important information needed to be taken from Earth to the All Alien Alliance or AAA. For frustrating reasons we stowed away on their motherfucking ship that looked like a clam with horns and a tail. Not exactly the best design winner in my book. When the mutant-clam-ship was attacked, I came up close and personal with a very sharp knife. One near-miss meeting with the grim reaper later, and I learned my dear psycho-pathic dad was still a total asshole trying to kill people. What's new? But, it's gotten worse and they need *my* help to stop him.

And, that is why, dear FIA, I'm heading back to Earth, on a small ship called D-ROMP, to deal with his sorry ass. Permanently. At least, that's *my* plan.

So, FIA—Can I call you FIA? Of course I can—you may be wondering how I'm coping with all of this. The answer is in your name.

Hey. I think I do feel a bit better. This might just be good for me after all. Look at me getting all therapized and in touch with my feels or some shit.

Fuck. It. All.
Spikey

D-ROMP, Space
October 21, 2025

One motherfucking bed! What the hell was she supposed to do now? No one had said anything about one goddamn bed. Jill stared into the only living space on the detachable rapid optimal maneuvering pod, also known as the D-ROMP, attempting not to panic. She didn't do panic, dammit. After everything she'd been through in her life, not one note of panic. Even with all the shit happening lately.

But this? This was taking things too far.

Find out how Jill decides to handle Nial and her one bed situation in Claiming Jill, which will be released in 2022.

ABOUT THE AUTHOR

Michelle Mars has an unhealthy obsession with coffee, caramel, and funny t-shirts. This single mom of two amazing, kind, and creative dragons/children has naturally purple hair and loves nothing more than talking books, kids, and living your best life. She enjoys reading romance, traveling, and writing stories that make her readers laugh, sweat, and swoon.

Author of the steamy, paranormal, sci-fi, rom-com Love Wars Series; Moving Jack, Chasing Rory, and Embracing Irina out now, and Claiming Jill, coming soon.

The first book in her contemporary rom-com series The Frisky Bean, Frisky Intentions, will be out in 2021 but you can catch a prequel short story named Frisky Connections in the Eight Kisses Hanukkah anthology out now.

Michelle's truth: Humor is a turn-on!

For updates go to www.michellemars.com and register to her newsletter.

facebook.com/michellemarsbooks

twitter.com/MichelleMarsHEA

instagram.com/michellemarsbooks

Moving Jack, Love Wars Book 1

You can buy the above cover in print signed by me from my website www. michellemars.com.

Chasing Rory, Love Wars Book 2

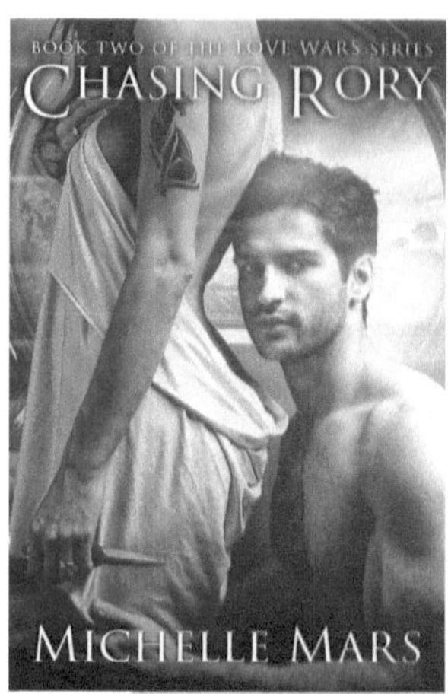

You can buy the above cover in print signed by me from my website www. michellemars.com.

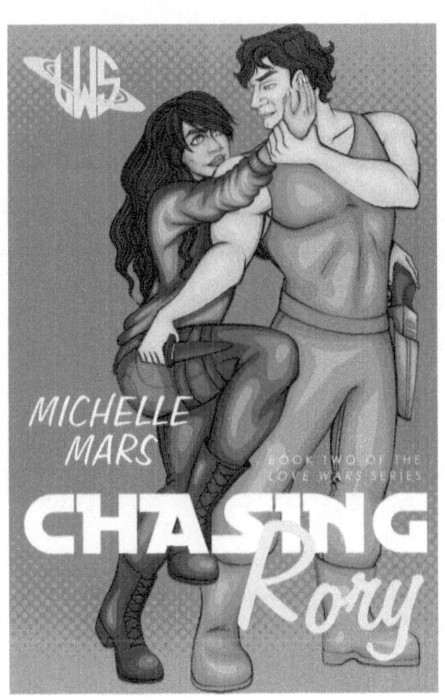
LWS
MICHELLE
MARS
BOOK TWO OF THE
LOVE WARS SERIES
CHASING
Rory